"You said you wanted to speak with me. What about?"

"This."

He kissed her. The kiss wasn't passionate or hard and demanding. Quite the opposite. It was a quiet, gentle touch of the lips. By the time Liz could register what had happened and react, the moment was over. Leaving her off balance.

"What…?" She was dazed. The words wouldn't form.

Charles smiled. "That's more like it," he said, the back of his hand reaching out to brush her cheek. "I've thought about doing that all night long."

A thousand butterflies chose that moment to take flight in her stomach. She pressed her palm flat against her abdomen to quell them.

Suddenly fascinated by the artwork hanging over his credenza, Liz walked toward it. "Do you always feel the need to kiss your secretaries?"

"Only the tall, feisty ones."

Dear Reader,

This book has a special place in my heart because it's the first time my heroine has had a child. As a mother myself, I understand the desire to give your child all the opportunities life has to offer. So often we as parents make sacrifices so that our kids can live their dreams. We sit through sports practices, we invest in tutors, we worry about their futures, etc. This is the world my heroine Liz Strauss lives in. Only she has it far tougher. As a single mother, she is not only a parent but the head of the household—which means dealing with all the day-to-day challenges that come with working and trying to maintain a home. On top of all that, she's carrying some pretty heavy baggage. No wonder she's ruled out romance!

Then there's Charles, my hero. There's something fun about taking a confident man and putting him in a world where he is completely out of his element. In this case he's transplanted into wintry New England, where hockey and slippery roads are the order of the day. Writing this story in the middle of a very snowy winter, I could totally identify with his desire to leave for warmer climates. Sometimes a little too much!

I loved taking these two characters, neither of whom is even thinking about falling in love, on a trip toward happily-ever-after. Deep down they are both such lonely souls. I was glad to play fictional matchmaker.

One other reason this book was so special is Liz's son Andrew. At this very moment the real-life Andrew will be waiting for his college admissions. It's not often a mother gets to capture her son's quirks and personality on the page. He was a good sport about the whole process.

As always, I love hearing from readers. Please contact me at Barbara@BarbaraWallace.com and tell me what you think!

Happy reading!

Barbara Wallace

BARBARA WALLACE
Daring to Date the Boss

TORONTO NEW YORK LONDON
AMSTERDAM PARIS SYDNEY HAMBURG
STOCKHOLM ATHENS TOKYO MILAN MADRID
PRAGUE WARSAW BUDAPEST AUCKLAND

Recycling programs
for this product may
not exist in your area.

ISBN-13: 978-0-373-74160-1

DARING TO DATE THE BOSS

First North American Publication 2012

Barbara Wallace is a lifelong romantic and daydreamer, so it's not surprising she decided to become a writer at the age of eight. However, it wasn't until a coworker handed her a romance novel that she knew where her stories belonged. For years she limited her dreams to nights, weekends and commuter train trips, while working as a communications specialist, PR freelancer and full-time mom. At the urging of her family she finally chucked the day job and pursued writing full-time—she couldn't be happier.

Barbara lives in Massachusetts with her husband, their teenage son and two very spoiled, self-centered cats (as if there could be any other kind). Readers can visit her at www.barbarawallace.com and find her on Facebook. She'd love to hear from you.

Books by Barbara Wallace

A FAIRYTALE CHRISTMAS
        "MAGIC UNDER THE MISTLETOE"
THE CINDERELLA BRIDE
THE HEART OF A HERO
BEAUTY AND THE BROODING BOSS

Other titles by this author available in ebook format.

To my family, as always,
for all their love and support.

And to the real Andrew, Victoria, and Sammy.
Thanks for being such great kids.

CHAPTER ONE

"Mom! Have you seen my history book?"

Liz Strauss let out a deep breath. She swore her son's baritone could be heard in the town house next door. "Where did you last use it?"

"If I knew that I wouldn't be asking."

Sure he would. Asking was so much easier than say, actually looking for the book. "Try next to the computer!" One of these days they would have to start communicating like normal people rather than hollering back and forth through rooms.

Today would not be that day. "Found it!" he called a moment later. "It was on the kitchen counter."

Near the food. Naturally. Crisis averted, for now, she returned to rehearsing her speech.

"Well, Mr. Bishop, as you know, my workload has increased since you arrived...."

Too whiny. She wanted to at least *sound*

smart and sophisticated, since looking that way appeared out of the question. Staring at her reflection, she smoothed some imaginary wrinkles from the front of her turtleneck. Her chin length bob clung to her head like a limp brown helmet. In trying to stave off static electricity, she'd overdosed on conditioner again. She looked like a drab, helmet-wearing dud.

Taking a deep breath, she resumed rehearsing. "Seeing as how my responsibilities have increased, I was hoping… No, I believe…" *Believe* was a much better word. "I *believe* I deserve…"

Why was this so hard? She'd been practicing since the shower, and still had no idea what she was going to say.

If Ron Bishop were still president, she'd simply say "Hey, Ron, Andrew has a chance to attend Trenton Academy, I need a raise to cover tuition."

Unfortunately she no longer worked for Ron, God rest his soul. No, she worked for his son, a man she'd never knew existed until three months ago. What did he care about private school tuition or opportunities of a lifetime? He was too busy decimating everything his father stood for.

On the other hand, she really did deserve a raise. Since arriving, Bishop had run her ragged. Then there was the steady stream of complaints caused by his new policies. Not a day went by that an angry manager didn't stop her to vent their frustrations. If you asked her, she deserved hazard pay for playing gatekeeper alone.

Maybe that should be her argument, she thought with a wry smile.

A small television sat on the corner of her bureau. On screen, a perky weatherwoman chirped about potential snowfall. *Her* bob, Liz noticed with annoyance, shimmered and swung under the studio lights as she waved her perfectly manicured hand in front of the map. "Depending on the storm's timing, we could be looking at a very messy evening commute," she said, sounding practically giddy.

When weren't they looking at a messy commute these days? Liz switched off the woman and her annoyingly bouncy hair. It was getting late. Rehearsal would have to wait.

As she padded down the stairs to the main

floor, Liz caught sight of the old juice stain marring the bottom step and did her best to quell her frustration. She had hoped to finally replace the old Berber carpeting this spring, but those plans would have to wait. She couldn't afford both home improvements and private school tuition. Heck, she could barely afford private school tuition alone unless she got this raise.

In the kitchen, her son, Andrew, was attempting to simultaneously stuff books in his backpack and half a bagel into his mouth. His six-foot-three frame and flailing arms took up most of the space, and she nearly had to duck to avoid being struck by a stray limb. He got his gangly height from her. Surprising their combined twelve feet could actually fit in the small space.

"One of these mornings you're going to choke," she remarked, grabbing a coffee mug from the open cupboard.

"Least then I wouldn't have to take my calculus exam," he shot back.

"Right, because death is always preferable to taking a test."

"This test, yes."

Calculus had been the bane of her son's

existence all year long. "Why? You studied, didn't you?"

Although partially hidden by floppy brown bangs, Liz caught his eye roll. "Like that matters. Mr. Rueben hates our entire class. He wants us to fail so he can have an excuse to yell at us."

Drama. Native language of the American teenager. Liz suppressed an eye roll of her own. "I'm sure he doesn't hate you. If you studied, you'll do fine."

Andrew took the coffee cup from her hand and washed down his bagel. "You always say that."

"And you always say you're going to fail. Score one for consistency." She snatched her coffee back. "Do you want me to pour you your own cup?"

"Don't have time. Vic's picking me up early so we can cram before school."

"Cram, huh?" A familiar lump dropped in the pit of her stomach. Victoria was a smart, sweet girl, she reminded herself. A nice girl.

A nice girl who had her own car and with whom her seventeen-year-old son was head over heels in love. Memories of backseats and misplaced teenage passion flashed before her eyes.

He's not you, Liz. So desperate to feel wanted, he'd toss the future away at the first sweet words of affection. From the moment she delivered him, she'd made sure Andrew never went a day feeling less than one hundred perfectly loved and wanted.

A car horn sounded outside.

"That's Vic," Andrew announced unnecessarily as he grabbed his bag. "See you after practice."

"Tell Victoria to drive carefully. The roads could get slippery later today."

"Yes, ma'am." Another eye roll. Wonder if he knew when he was doing it, or if the gesture was automatic, like breathing.

"Hey, sue me for not wanting my only child hurt in a car accident," she told him.

"If it would get me out of this exam..."

"Don't even joke about it, mister." She silenced him with a wag of her index finger. "Good luck on your test. And be—"

He was out the door before she could finish the sentence.

Mug gripped between her hands, Liz fought the urge to watch and make sure they pulled out of her driveway safely. Andrew wasn't a little boy anymore. He didn't need his mother hovering like a helicopter, watching his every move. Knowing so, however, didn't make cutting the cord any easier.

Time moved way too fast. Seemed like only yesterday he was a seven-year-old clamoring to stay up past eight o'clock. Now here he was on the cusp of adulthood with a chance, if the Trenton hockey coach was to be believed, to earn a scholarship to a major university. Barring any stupid mistakes, her job was almost finished. She'd done good, she decided. Better than her parents. Then again, they hadn't set the bar all that high, had they?

Out of the corner of her eye, she caught her reflection in the microwave. How was it possible that her hair got flatter from the time she left the bedroom until now? Tipping her head upside down, she tried fluffing the strands with her fingers like they did at the hair salon. All that did was make her hair look like a static-laden mushroom.

Good thing she was banking on her efficiency and not her looks to charm her boss. As if the man could be charmed by anything but a spreadsheet anyway. Most of the employees were convinced he was some kind of walking computer.

Maybe that's what she should do. Lay out her arguments in a spreadsheet and shove the paper under his nose. Then she wouldn't have to worry about her hair or anything else.

Chuckling to herself, Liz sipped her coffee. If she thought the idea would actually work, she would. In the meantime, she'd better figure out what she was going to say to convince her boss to give her a raise. Andrew was going to Trenton Academy next year come hell or high water. He'd gone without enough in his short life. Her baby boy would have all the opportunities she never had, no matter what. Even if she had to beg, borrow or steal to do so. Today she planned on begging.

Hopefully Charles Bishop felt like giving.

Liz had planned on arriving at the office extra early to allow herself time to compose before making her request. Unfortunately she got stuck behind the middle-school bus and had to endure stopping every five minutes through downtown Gilmore and extra early didn't happen. In fact, plain old regular early barely happened. As she slipped out of her wool coat and fired up her computer, Liz wondered if she would even have time to catch her breath. She hoped to make her request first thing, before Bishop got engrossed in those spreadsheets he loved so much.

Maybe she'd luck out and he'd get stuck in traffic, too. Although then he might be in a bad mood, and she didn't want that, either.

"Good morning, Elizabeth."

Drat. He'd arrived on time. Figures.

Flashing her best professional smile, she reached behind her and retrieved a sheet of paper from the printer. "Good morning. I was about to put today's itinerary on your desk."

As usual, the new CEO of Bishop Paper looked like a million dollars. Or multimillion, if Liz was to be accurate. Cashmere overcoat, designer wool suit, custom-cut shirt. He looked as natural standing in the no-nonsense offices as a marble sculpture at a flea market. His features, chiseled by anyone's standards, were dark and somber as he slipped the itinerary from her hand.

"Did Accounting deliver the revenue projections yet?" he asked, eyes scanning the schedule.

More spreadsheets. The man was definitely obsessed. "Not yet," she replied.

He raised his eyes to focus on her. Though she hated herself for it, Liz's breath caught. Framed by black lashes so lush it wasn't fair, her boss's cobalt eyes glistened like a pair of bright blue marbles. It wasn't fair that a man so cold and irritating in every other aspect had eyes like that. Why couldn't he have plain old boring eyes like normal people?

"Tell them I'd like the numbers emailed to me by ten o'clock," he told her. "I want to review them before our meeting this afternoon."

"Sure thing." She'd wait until he went into his office before delivering the bad news. Leanne, the VP's secretary, was going to have a fit, and her rants could get loud. Another reason she deserved a pay raise. To compensate for the potential hearing loss.

"I'm also expecting an overnight package from Xinhua Paper," he continued. "Bring it in as soon as it arrives."

With his business complete, her boss moved toward his office door. Liz's palms began to sweat. It was now or never. "I was wondering…" She began.

Hand already on his office door, he paused. His eyes turned in her direction again, causing another skip in her breath. "Yes?"

"Could I have a few moments of your time? I have something I'd like to discuss with you."

He frowned. "Something wrong?"

"No, nothing's wrong." Well, nothing but her salary. "I just wanted to ask you something. Job-related," she felt compelled to add.

"All right." Liz would have felt better if his response hadn't sounded put upon. "Let's go into my office."

His office. Three months and it still sounded strange to hear him refer to his father's domain that way. Yet every time Liz crossed the threshold, she got a hard reminder that Ron Bishop wasn't coming back. While alive, the former CEO filled his office shelves with photos from company events and fundraisers. Shots of him golfing in Bermuda with vendors. A picture of him grilling burgers at the company barbecue. Another of him cheering with staff members at a Boston baseball game.

There hadn't been a single picture of his son, however.

Charles removed the photos the day he

arrived. His idea of decorating consisted of bound data reports. The only vaguely personal item in the room was the super expensive coffeemaker on the corner credenza. The man could leave tomorrow and you'd never know he'd been there.

She waited while he hung up his coat. "What is it you wanted to discuss?"

Liz smoothed the front of her turtleneck, pausing to lay her palm flat against her stomach. "As you know, since you took over, my workload has increased. Not that I'm complaining," she quickly reassured him.

He'd crossed to the credenza and was measuring coffee beans into the built-in grinder. "Glad to hear it." There was a brief whirr and the coffeemaker started up. Liz had to raise her voice to continue.

"I realize when a company changes management, the transition brings a lot of additional work and that having been Ron's administrative assistant for ten years, I'm the best conduit between you and the rest of the company as far as information goes."

Good Lord, did that even make sense?

The grinding ceased making the room quiet once more. Charles pressed Brew. "And?"

Liz paused and took a deep breath. Go big or go home. Isn't that what Andrew and his hockey buddies always said? "And, given my extra workload, I was hoping you'd consider reexamining my salary."

"You want a raise."

"Yes, I do."

The room was silent except for the gurgling drip of the coffeemaker. Charles walked to his desk. With methodical precision, he removed his smart phone from his breast pocket, then slipped off his suit jacket and hung it over the back of his chair. Finally he rolled up his sleeves, smoothing each crisp fold. Liz felt like someone had started practicing slap shots in her stomach.

"You already make a pretty good salary," he finally replied, sitting down. "More than the other administrative assistants on staff."

"Yes, but I also do more than the other administrative assistants," she countered. "Not to mention I put in far more hours. I work late. I bring work home. I come in weekends. In fact, in many companies my position would be considered more than a simple administrative assistant." She was fudging that last part. But didn't Ron always say he couldn't run the company without her?

"No one's questioning your dedication, Elizabeth. Or your value to the company."

Good. Could it be she'd worried for nothing? Although the tiny voice in her head urged otherwise, a small seed of hope took root. She watched as Charles leaned back in his chair, the tips of his long fingers pressed together. "However, I'm in the process of cutting costs. There's a freeze on all reviews and pay increases."

"I know." She'd typed the memo. "I was hoping you would consider making an exception, given the circumstances."

"If I make an exception for you, I have to make an exception for everyone."

Her hope withered and died. "I'm not looking for a huge increase. It's just that my son—"

"Not at the present time, Elizabeth." He cut off her argument before she got started. "You can revisit the issue at your next performance review. In the meantime, I'm sorry."

Sorry, her foot. He wasn't sorry about anything except her wasting his precious time.

For the first time since she started as a file clerk, Liz hated where she worked.

Correction. For the first time, she hated the man she worked for.

That same man was reaching for his phone, effectively dismissing her and her request like lint from his expensive slacks. "Make sure accounting gets me those numbers by ten," he said, without looking up.

Liz didn't respond. Why bother? He wouldn't listen anyway. The arrogant, numbers-obsessed, heartless, penny-pinching, arrogant...

She marched straight from the office to the ladies' room, running out of adjectives halfway there. Furious, she kicked the door open. Pain shot from her toe to her knee.

Good. Gave her an excuse for being teary-eyed should anyone ask. Because she absolutely refused to give her boss the satisfaction of seeing her upset. No, she would be strong and stoic and all those other great New England traits. Too bad stoic couldn't erase feeling like she'd been punched.

No one's questioning your dedication or your workload. The comment mockingly repeated itself in her head. That was her mistake, she realized, dabbing at her mascara. Getting her hopes up when she heard the compliment. When was she going to learn? Compliments, sweet-talk, promises—none of them meant a thing.

Now what was she going to do? Tell An drew he wouldn't be attending Trenton Academy after all? He'd been so excited about the opportunity. *Their players get recruited by Division I schools, Mom. Wouldn't that be cool if I could play for BU or Harvard?* Attending a school like Trenton could open so many doors for Andrew. Doors she never had the chance to even look at. She'd be darned if her son didn't get every opportunity.

Of course, thanks to her boss, she would have to find another way to open those doors. Maybe Bill… Right. She nixed that idea out of the box. Andrew's father hadn't come through in seventeen years. Why on earth would he come through now?

Like always, she was on her own.

Damn Charles Bishop and his belt tightening. She hoped he choked.

"First thing tomorrow morning, James. I'm not paying your firm a retainer to procrastinate." Hanging up, Charles swiveled around in his chair to face the window. Outside, a few stray flakes had begun to fall, their crystal shapes disappearing amidst the blanket of white covering the ground. Off in the distance, the White Mountains disappeared into the gray mist. Gray-white peaks crisscrossed with rock and ski trails.

He couldn't believe he was back in New Hampshire. After all these years, he'd thought the Granite State was forever in his past. A distant, unwelcome memory. Yet here he was, back in Gilmore, saddled with his father's beloved company. The lawyers suggested the inheritance was a final conciliatory gesture, a chance to fix in death what he left broken in life. "Consider it Ron's way of making amends," he'd said.

Charles couldn't care less what the reason was. His father hadn't wanted him; he didn't want his father's blasted company. Clearly, the old man chose the wrong legacy to hang his hat on. Far as he was concerned Bishop Paper was nothing more than another acquisition in a long line of acquisitions. Companies to be turned over as quickly and profitably as possible.

A soft knock sounded on his door. Turning, he saw Elizabeth in his doorway, looking like a beige turtleneck-wearing will-o'-the-wisp. She cleared her throat, the sound immediately calling attention to red-rimmed eyes, evidence of a ladies' room meltdown. No doubt she despised him. Or despised him more, as the case may be, since he was pretty sure he'd been abhorred by everyone since day one. Ice King. Wasn't that what they referred to him as behind his back? Fairly apropos, if you asked him. Certainly his insides felt numb enough.

To his assistant's credit, her reddened eyes were the only evidence of distress. She maintained a steely expression as she approached, her low-heeled pumps crossing neatly one ankle in front of the other.

"Your package from Xinhua," she clipped. A flash of veiled contempt passed across her features as she handed him the thick envelope. Definitely despised him. "Will there be anything else?" she asked.

"Not at the moment," he replied.

Turning on her heel, she strode from the room. Briefly Charles watched her depart, noting how her newly acquired stiffness gave her backside an attractive sway. She'd probably loathe him even more if she knew that's what he was thinking, he thought, corner of his mouth ticking upward.

Once the door clicked shut, he turned his attention to the package in his hands. Huang Bin was nothing if not prompt in his reply.

He'd known from day one, the key to unloading his albatross of an inheritance would lay in Asia. The heydays of New England paper manufacturing were over. For a medium-size manufacturer like Bishop to survive, it needed either an owner dedicated long-term to its success or a parent company large enough it didn't care about the location. And since Charles had zero interest in whether Bishop lived or died…

Fortunately for him, Xinhua Paper was interested in establishing a toehold in America. Soon as legally possible, he planned on selling. Closing the book on Bishop Paper once and for all.

By lunchtime, Liz felt moderately better. All, she conceded, was not lost. There were plenty of ways she could swing tuition. She could get a second job, look into a longer term loan.

Or beg Trenton's financial aid office for more money. Their ears couldn't be any more deaf than the man she worked for.

"Who died?" asked Leanne Kenny. The accounting secretary walked into the break room. *Bustled* was a more apt word. Her square, stocky build made any other adjective inadequate.

"My credit score," Liz replied. "Think charging an entire year of school tuition would be a problem?"

"Still trying to get your son into Trenton, huh?" Reaching into the fridge, the older woman pulled out a set of plastic storage containers filled with salad fixings. "You know, going to public school is hardly the end of the world."

"I know." Liz also knew Leanne thought her a snob for wanting otherwise. Like most of the rank and file at the company, her colleague sent her children to Gilmore High and couldn't understand why Liz felt so strongly about this. She didn't understand that for Liz, sending Andrew to Trenton wasn't about the quality of education. Of course he would do just fine at the town high school.

Of course, explaining her reasons would

mean going into the sordid details of her mis-spent youth, something she wasn't about to do. Bad enough simple math told part of the story for her.

She changed the subject instead. "Thanks for getting those reports out this morning. Mr. Bishop was eager to get them."

"He's always eager," Leanne grumbled. She poured a container of creamy dressing over her bowl of lettuce. "Man's definitely not his father. Ron believed in giving people notice."

True, Liz thought to herself. She tore off a bite of peanut butter sandwich. Interesting how they all referred to Ron by his first name while his son received the more formal address. Then, they'd known Ron. Most of them had worked for the man for years. Unlike Charles, who they didn't know at all. Their new boss went out of his way to keep his distance.

Like a king in his tower, she thought, this morning's bitterness returning.

"What is his fascination with spreadsheets anyway?" Leanne was asking. "I swear he demands a different report every day."

"The man does like his numbers." Probably looking for more costs to cut.

Leanne leaned forward, her eyes shining like a little girl with a secret. "Paul in Human Resources told me he's cutting the company barbecue. Said that if we wanted to 'play family'—" she framed the words with air quotes "—we could do so on our own time. Talk about harsh."

Harsh indeed. Obviously Charles Bishop was determined to eke out every penny of profit he could out of the company, employees' welfare be damned. How could a man be so different from his father? In this case, the apple hadn't just fallen far from the tree, it had rolled into the next state.

A noise in the doorway caused them both to jump. Since Charles took over, the entire company was on edge, with everyone waiting for the next big bombshell. As if Ron's death hadn't been big enough. To both their relief, Van Hancock and Doug Metcalf, two of the company's sales managers, walked in. Their down coats glistened with droplets of melting snow.

"You talking about the new boss?" Van asked, brushing dampness from his gray crew cut.

"Shh," Leanne said. "Not so loud."

"Sorry." He dropped his voice a notch. "So what did the Ice King do now?"

"Cut the employee barbecue."

"Not surprising," Van replied. "He's cut everything else."

"Wonder how long before he sells this place?" Doug wondered aloud. "I mean, isn't that what he does?"

"According to the articles online," said Leanne. "No reason to think this company will be any different."

Thinking of the overnight package from China, Liz stayed silent. Annoyed as she was with her boss, she had no intention of giving away proprietary information. Office gossip wasn't her style. Never had been. Though she might have indulged in a little Internet surfing when Charles came onboard. That was for research purposes however. One should know who she worked for, and seeing as how no one had ever heard Ron talk about his son before…

"Makes you wonder what Ron was thinking when he wrote up his will," the accounting secretary continued, stuffing a piece of lettuce in her mouth.

"Maybe he thought this time would be different," Doug offered. "Because it's a family business and all."

"Yeah right," she scoffed. "Did any of you even know Ron had a son?"

"I heard him mention something once," Van said in between bites of his cheeseburger.

Hearing the remark, Liz looked up. Like most of them, she'd had no clue Ron Bishop and Charles Bishop, corporate raider, were related until Charles arrived on their doorstep. "What did he say?"

"Not much," the salesman replied with a shrug. "It was when my eldest was looking at colleges a couple years ago. Said something about his son having gone to some technical school. I was surprised because I'd forgotten he'd been married. Had to have been twenty-five years or so since his divorce."

"I didn't even know that much," Doug replied.

Neither had Liz. She and Ron had worked side by side for a decade and he'd never mentioned anything. That stung. She'd thought they'd been close, especially since his heart attack. But then, it wouldn't be the first time she'd misjudged a relationship, would it?

"Maybe the subject was too painful," she murmured, grasping for a reason.

"I bet," Leanne said as she stabbed another piece of lettuce. "Poor Ron. I miss him." The two men nodded in agreement. "This place will never be the same."

"No, it won't," a frosty baritone replied.

All four of them froze. You could hear a pin drop in the silence.

Liz looked up first, her eyes connecting with Charles's. He stood leaning against the door frame, shoulder propped, hands in pockets. He would have presented quite the nonchalant picture were it not for the sharp glint behind his blue stare. No idea how much Charles heard, but he'd clearly heard enough.

Guilty warmth crept into Liz's cheeks.

He didn't move a muscle. Not even a tick. "I'm sure the West Coast customers are open by now," he said to Van and Doug.

Bravado gone, both men, along with Leanne, quickly gathered their belongings. Liz moved to follow suit. She was halfway to the trash receptacle when his low voice halted her progress.

"A moment, Elizabeth."

Drat. Three sets of feet could be heard hustling away like rats deserting a ship. Leaving her and Charles alone.

Squaring her shoulders, she deliberately finished disposing of her leftovers before turning around, feeling Charles's gaze every inch of the way. "Yes?" she asked when she finished.

He pushed himself away from the wall. "I realize whenever there's a change in leadership, a company goes through growing pains and an amount of gossip is to be expected." His voice was soft, measured. "Particularly when the change is sudden and unexpected.

"However." He paused, leveling his blue gaze straight at her. Liz instinctively swallowed hard. "However," he repeated, "I expect a certain level of discretion—and loyalty—from my personal assistant. In the future, I'd appreciate if you refrain from watercooler gossip."

Liz's spine stiffened. In her palm, she held an apple, leftover from her lunch, and she squeezed the fruit tightly, her fingers crushing the pulp. Humiliation flushed through her, but she choked the feeling back. Tilting her chin, she met his stare head-on, for the first time grateful for her height as it forced her to look down her nose. "Is there anything else, Mr. Bishop?" she asked matching his measured tone.

An unidentifiable expression ghosted across his features. "No, that'll be all. For now."

"Then I'll get back to my desk." Palming her apple, she walked past, keeping her head high the entire time.

And pretending she couldn't feel his eyes watching her every step.

True to meteorologists' word, the storm peaked during the evening commute. What had been steady but light snow all day had become a blanket of white, obliterating all but a few feet of visibility.

Downshifting for God knows what time, Charles leaned back against the headrest and groaned. By this point in the winter, shouldn't people know how to drive in snow? Weren't New Englanders supposed to be of sturdier stock? Steely backbone and all that?

More like his secretary, he thought, mood lifting slightly. Elizabeth had surprised him today—twice actually—with her shows of resolve. Looked like there was a little mettle in that extra long spine of hers. Funny how he'd never noticed before.

The discovery was the sole bright spot in what was otherwise a very long day. His morning accounting meeting turned into a daylong argument, filled with defensive posturing and excuses. Each angry glare conveyed the same silent message. You are not your father.

Damn straight, he'd wanted to say. Better get used to it.

Ahead, the road dipped and followed the trees lining the Androscoggin River. The car in front of him stopped suddenly, forcing him to step on the brakes. There was a sliding sensation as Charles's car fishtailed toward a row of pines, and he quickly steered it back under control. His two-seat Italian sports car wasn't suited for winter driving. He should garage the thing in favor of a sturdier vehicle with four-wheel drive, but a stubborn part of him refused. Doing so would be like giving in to his exile. Acknowledging he was settling in New Hampshire for a long stay and that was decidedly not the case. Hell, he was already getting restless. Unusually so. He'd felt unsettled, antsy, on edge since getting the news about his father. Maybe it was being back in New Hampshire.

Or maybe it was simply all the cold and snow, he thought, watching the blades trek back and forth across his windshield. Hard to believe once upon a time, he saw the stuff as something almost magical.

Look, Daddy! I built a snowman!

Not now, Charles. I'm busy.

Charles closed off the memory. His snowman-making days were long gone. Now all he wanted was to get back to his condo, fix himself a martini and catch the evening stock report. Given the day, maybe even two martinis—

Son of a—! Brown flashed in front of his windshield. Charles slammed on the brakes, yanking his steering wheel harder to the right to avoid collision. His car began to spin. There was another flash of brown. A flailing of hooves against metal and glass followed by a jolt and a loud bang.

Then, nothing.

CHAPTER TWO

THE more Liz thought about her little dress-down in the break room, the more irritated she became until by the drive home, her teeth hurt from grinding them. Fortunately the Ice King spent the bulk of the afternoon holed up in an accounting meeting, leaving her to work in peace. The nerve of him, singling her out. Then, worst of all, he had the audacity to flash her a condescending smile on his way out the door. *I expect a certain amount of discretion and loyalty...* Unbelievable.

Okay, so they shouldn't have been talking about him in the break room. But did he really think he could waltz in and turn the entire company on its ear without repercussion? That employees were going to simply sit back and say nothing during this—what did he call it? This difficult transition. What kind of person refers to his father's death as a transition anyway?

The kind who didn't have anything to do with him while he was alive, that's who.

She turned out of the parking lot. The narrow wooded road that led from the manufacturing facilities into downtown was unusually busy. Just her luck. School bus this morning, snow backup tonight. No telling how long getting home would take.

Keeping her hands securely planted on the steering wheel at ten and two, she arched her back. Her shoulders and neck ached with tension as much as her jaw, and the notion that Andrew was home alone with Victoria didn't help. They were "doing homework" his text message said. She hoped that's all they were "doing."

If Ron were still alive, she'd have asked to take off early to avoid the traffic congestion, a concept his son would certainly reject, even though he departed before her. Did she ever miss her old boss. Ron had cared about his employees. Especially the last few years following his first heart attack. Bishop Paper is my family, he used to tell her. Knowing his biological family wanted nothing to do with him gave those words a whole new meaning, didn't it? Liz rubbed her neck, trying to shake off the disquieting prickle. Again, she thought to herself, why? Far as she could see, the fault had to lie with Charles. Clearly the man lacked the ability for human empathy.

Besides, she knew what neglectful parents looked like. They were tired and ignorant and forced their children to look for love in the backseat of a sedan, tossing them out when the search backfired. They weren't zesty and fun-loving and they didn't leave their children multimillion dollar companies.

Rounding the corner, the traffic changed from slow to a snail's pace. Squinting, Liz could just make out the bright flashing lights of emergency vehicles.

A few minutes later, as the traffic crawled closer, she saw the reason. A red sports car, nose-first in a snowbank. Only one person in town drove such an impractical and expensive car. Sure enough, Charles's dark familiar figure stood glowering at a police officer while a tow driver hooked a chain to the underside of his car. Fortunately, he looked unscathed; the EMT was already preparing to leave.

Liz couldn't help her satisfaction. Served

him right for driving the darn thing in the first place. With any luck, he'd be stuck standing in the snow a good long time, too. Till his outsides got as cold as his blood.

As she approached, Charles turned and looked in her direction, almost as if he sensed her approach. Probably her aging muffler. Either way, his eyes reached through the windshield, catching hers and for a moment, everything else faded away except for their silvery-blue reflection in her headlights.

Aw, drat; he was her boss after all. Before she had time to reconsider Liz had stopped and rolled down her window.

"What happened?" she asked him.

"A blasted deer is what happened. Damn thing bolted in front of my car."

Liz wished she could say she was surprised, but she wasn't. Collisions with deer were fairly common on these roads. Charles was lucky the accident hadn't been worse. "Are you all right?"

"He hit his head, but refused medical treatment," the officer said.

"The air bag hit me," Charles snapped in correction, "and I'm fine." Despite his objections, Liz caught the hint of a shake as his hand combed through his curls. "Wish I could say the same for my car." A few feet away, the tow crane started up. The sound of crunching metal could be heard above the wind, causing him to wince. "More so now," he muttered.

Meanwhile, the snow had begun falling even heavier. Flakes covered the shoulders of Charles's black coat. When they weren't raking through his hair, his hands were jammed deep in his pockets, and while his features were partially obscured by shadows, Liz suspected his cheeks were blown raw from standing in the harsh northeastern wind. To her surprise, she actually felt sympathetic. "Do you need a ride?"

Hearing the question, he looked as caught off guard as she did when asking. He looked to the police officer. "Do you need anything else?"

The man shook his head. "You can get a copy of the report from the station tomorrow for your insurance. And I'd reconsider having your doctor look you over. Whiplash doesn't always show its effects right away."

Charles nodded, but Liz could tell from experience, he was simply agreeing to end the conversation, that he had no intention of seeing a doctor. His father used to make the same expression.

Interesting. It was the first she'd seen a resemblance between the two men.

It wasn't until Charles retrieved his belongings and slid into the passenger seat that Liz questioned being a Good Samaritan. Normally she considered her SUV, chosen to accommodate her, Andrew and a ton of hockey equipment, to be quite comfortable. But somehow, with Charles riding shotgun, the space suddenly felt filled to capacity. She could feel every ounce of his presence buttressing her personal space. For someone who'd been standing out in the cold, he gave off a lot of body heat. The subtle scent of citrus and spice clung to the air, which had grown strangely close despite the large size cab. Gave her the overwhelming urge to shift in her seat. She wondered if Charles noticed the discomfort, too, because both his body and voice were stiff as he clipped his thank-you.

"You're welco— Oh my gosh, your cheek!" Under the illumination of the dome light, she could see the red slash of a friction burn marring his cheekbone. "You really did hit your head," she said, instinctively reaching to check closer. Her fingertips brushed across his stubble. "Maybe you should get that checked out."

"It's nothing." He shrugged off her touch, and Liz suddenly realized what she'd done. "Sorry," she replied, yanking her hand back. "Maternal habit. I'm forever checking my son's injuries."

Oh, drat, Andrew! She was going to be later than ever now. What had she been thinking? Quickly she reached for her pocketbook.

Charles eyed her. "What are you doing?"

"Texting my son."

"You have children?"

He sounded surprised. That would make him the only person at Bishop Paper who didn't know. "A son. He's almost... I want to let him know I'm delayed but will be home soon."

"Considerate of you."

Again, his voice sounded off, like he didn't quite believe her. "I don't want him to worry," she replied, pressing Send. On the other hand, now he'd realize he had extra time. Why if it were she and Bill and they had an extra fifteen minutes…

Andrew wasn't her. And Victoria wasn't Bill. She needed to remember that.

She must have frowned at her phone, though, because Charles immediately asked, "Is there a problem?"

"Signal's patchy. My message isn't going through." That'll teach her for going with the cheapest carrier. "It's all right. I'm sure he's heard on the radio about the bad commute. He'll be fine." He and Victoria.

"No offense, but your acting skills need a little work."

"It's fine." If he could snap, so could she. "Nothing I can't handle."

Out of the corner of her eye, she saw the tow truck pulling out into the traffic. She turned on her directional and pulled out behind it. Now that she'd gotten herself into driving him home, she might as well get to it. "Thirty-two Greengus Street, right?" She remembered Ron's address from company events.

"No. I'm staying at the Admiral Mill Complex."

Liz knew the place. The old textile facilities had been refurbished into condominiums last year. Still, she'd assumed he'd stay at his father's house. After all, he did own it now.

"I'm having the house renovated for re-sale," he replied, reading her mind. "And I prefer my own space," he added, turning toward the window.

"Well, from what I gather, the mill has a lot of it."

"Yes, it does."

They drove the next mile or so in silence. Liz did her best to watch the snow and the traffic, but the man next to her kept drawing her attention. She'd never realized how well sound carried when the radio wasn't blasting. In the stillness, every breath, every soft swish of his coat across his slacks echoed voluminously. Painfully aware of his proximity, she held her own space as close to her as possible, keeping her elbows tight to her body and willing her angles and limbs to stay narrow. Worse, he didn't seem to notice how much space he took up.

Not even when his sleeve brushed up against her side pocket, causing a shiver to course through her entire body.

"You can relax, you know. Despite what

you all think, I'm not the devil incarnate. I won't bite."

Okay, maybe he was more aware than she realized. "I know."

"Is that so? Again, your acting skills, Elizabeth. You're a terrible liar."

No, he was a terrible passenger. "I'm giving you a ride home, aren't I? Why would I do that if I thought you were so evil?"

"You tell me."

Entering downtown Gilmore, they passed the town common and St. Mark's Episcopal Church whose tall white steeple rose up and disappeared in the snowy sky. A poster board sign on the lawn advertised the upcoming hockey pancake breakfast in Gilmore High blue and gold.

Liz felt Charles's eyes studying her. "You know," he said finally, "at least a dozen other employees passed by the accident site. None of them stopped."

"None of them are your secretary."

"Interesting. I didn't realize chauffeur was part of your job description."

"Guess I'm a woman of many hats." Not that she was being paid for them all, she noted silently.

"Appears so. Secretary. Chauffeur. Office confidante."

He meant the discussion he interrupted in the break room. Frustration flashed anew. "For your information, I take my position seriously." No matter how much she disliked her boss. "I do not share company secrets."

"Good to know. Because I need to trust the people who work directly for me."

"Runs both ways."

"Excuse me? Did you say something?"

She hadn't realized she'd spoken aloud. Her cheeks warmed. "Nothing," she replied, eyes staying glued to the road.

"'Nothing' sounded an awful lot like a complaint. If you have something on your mind, I'd like to know."

Liz heard the rustle of fabric. Without looking she knew he'd shifted in his seat and now sat regarding her closely. The scrutiny had her pinned to the spot. "Elizabeth? Your thoughts?"

If she didn't know better, she'd say there was a note of humor in the way he prodded her. Like he wanted her to argue with him. She shrugged, hoping her answer would come across as nonchalant. "I doubt anything I have to say will be of interest to you."

"Why don't you let me be the judge?"

Right. And then her opinions could come back and bite her. She'd been reprimanded and rejected enough for one day, thank you very much.

"If you don't mind, I'll pass."

"You're worried about repercussions."

"Do you blame me?" she asked, casting him another look.

"I give you my word."

"Yeah, well like you said, trust has to be earned."

Charles chuckled.

"I wasn't trying to be funny," she told him.

"I know. I was actually thinking your remark was…" He paused. "Well-aimed."

An odd choice of words. "Thank you." She guessed.

"I take it that's your way of saying the employees don't trust me."

"They don't know what to expect. First your father dies unexpectedly and then you show up. You have to understand, until a few months ago, no one even knew you existed."

"I know." Charles's voice was hard and flat

and a tad too unaffected. She felt a stirring of sympathy, which disturbed her, because he was supposed to be the bad guy.

"People miss him," she said simply. "He was an integral part of our lives and now he's gone."

"Employers come and go all the time, Elizabeth. It's how the business works."

For Charles, sure. After all, he made his living rotating in and out company doors. Not Ron, though. "Your father considered the company family. That's how he treated us."

"I'm sure he did."

Once again Liz felt the unanticipated swirl of sympathy.

To her relief, a large black and silver sign rose into view, announcing the entrance to Admiral Mill. Liz took the turn like she was entering heaven. "Here you go. Safe and sound." And not a minute too soon, she added to herself. Today had been a roller coaster of a day, this drive being the last in a string of undesired and abnormal interactions with her boss. One second she's furious with him, the next she's feeling sympathy and fussing over the mark on his cheek. It was a schizophrenic mix and frankly she had a headache from all the different reactions he'd put her through. The sooner he stepped out of her car the better.

Which, from the way his hand was on the handle, looked to be imminent. "Thank you for your assistance," he told her.

"All in a day's work. Good night, Mr. Bishop."

"Good night, Elizabeth. I'll see you tomorrow morning. Shall we say, seven? I'd like to get an early start."

Liz blinked. Early start? "Um, sure?"

"Good. The gate will be unlocked so you'll have no trouble getting in. If I'm not out front, buzz the penthouse and I'll be right down."

"Buzz the penthouse," Liz repeated. She wanted to make sure she heard him right. "You expect me to drive you tomorrow?"

"I'm not sure how else I'm going to get to Concord. I have a meeting at the State House regarding the new environmental regs, remember?"

Of course she remembered. She'd set up the meeting. She hadn't expected to drive him there is all. When she opened her mouth to say so, he did something unexpected.

He smiled.

A damnably sexy off-kilter grin that arched his brow and, had it truly reached his eyes, would melt the insides of every woman in town. "Well, you did say chauffeur was in your job description."

The Charles Bishop roller-coaster ride was officially plummeting. His driver. He actually expected her to cart him to Concord tomorrow morning for a meeting.

"Arrgh!" Letting out a groan, Liz smashed her palm against the steering wheel. She didn't know what angered her more—her boss blithely assuming she'd do his bidding or her agreeing like some weak-kneed imbecile.

"Can't you rent a car?" she'd asked.

"The rental agency is two towns away, and I doubt very much it's open," he'd replied. "In case you didn't notice, it's snowing."

She'd noticed. The foolish snow was what got her into this predicament. She should have left him standing on the side of the road.

In the end, she'd had no choice but to concede. She liked getting a regular paycheck, no matter how small. And much as she hated to admit, he had a point about the businesses being closed until morning.

So she agreed to pick him up at seven o'clock. That didn't mean, however, she was happy about the task. Or that she was at all charmed by that sexy cockeyed smile he tried tossing in her direction.

Andrew and Victoria were curled up watching a movie when she unlocked the door. Her son barely looked up. "What happened? I thought you said fifteen minutes," he said. "You took forty-five. Your text said you'd be home in fifteen minutes."

"Mr. Bishop hit a deer and wrecked his car. I had to drive him home. I tried to send a text but the storm's messing with a signal. Were you worried?"

"No, I've been waiting to eat. I'm starved. Ow! What?" Rubbing his shoulder, he looked over at his girlfriend.

"Be nice to your mother," Victoria said.

"Listen to your girlfriend." Liz hung up her coat. "Do your parents know you're here?"

The young blonde nodded. "My dad said he'd come pick me up when he finished plowing out my grandmother's driveway. He didn't want me driving in the snow."

"Good idea." Though a better one might have been to have her go home straight after school. She studied the two teenagers sitting on the sofa. Victoria's long blond hair spilled over onto Andrew's shoulder. Did they have to invade each other's personal space constantly? Even when they weren't touching they were touching.

Kind of like driving in the car with Charles. The thought brought a warm unwelcome shiver.

"What's the new Mr. Bishop like?" Victoria asked. "One of my mom's customers said he was gorgeous. Hey!" This time she rubbed her shoulder.

"Andrew, don't poke your girlfriend. And yes, you could say he was good-looking." If lacking any kind of human feelings.

Unless you counted his smile. Or the wounded tone he tried to hide in his voice.

Kicking off her wet shoes, Liz padded her way toward the kitchen.

"I told Vic she could stay for dinner," Andrew called after her. "Is that all right?"

"Of course. She's always welcome. Have her call her father, though, so he knows."

"See," he said, poking his girlfriend with his elbow. "I told you she'd say yes."

That was her. Ms. Pushover. Word must have gotten around. "Hope spaghetti's all right with you two." She opened the cupboard and began pulling out the saucepans. "Do me a favor, Andrew. Check the freezer and see if we have any garlic bread, will you?" Nothing like garlic bread to keep the good-night kissing to a minimum. "How'd your calculus test go?"

"It went."

"Went good or bad?"

"It just went. By the way—" Andrew lumbered over to the fridge "—the furnace started making that weird noise again. Oh, and Mrs. Warren finished my recommendation for Trenton. You have no idea how badly I wanted to sneak a look, but she sealed the envelope. I put it in the folder with the application stuff. Oh, and Coach said he'd have something for me by the weekend."

Liz managed an acknowledging smile. Was it only this morning she asked for a raise? "Great, sweetie."

"I still can't believe you're going to Trenton," Victoria said. "You're not going to turn into some rich snob are you?"

"Of course I am. I'm going to be the star player. Everyone's going to love me— Ow! She poked me again. How come you never yell at her?"

"Because I like her better," Liz replied by rote. She was busy pretending to draw water from the faucet. Soon as Andrew mentioned the furnace, she got a sick feeling in her stomach. It had been acting up all fall. She'd put off calling a repairman because she feared a big bill. Hopefully she could string things out a little longer. Thanks to today's rejection, she really couldn't afford any large expenses. Not if she wanted to pay Andrew's tuition to Trenton. And—she glanced at the two teenagers giggling a few feet away—she so wanted to give Andrew this chance.

Meanwhile, her head ached from going three rounds with Charles Bishop and she had to repeat the process tomorrow. Driving to Concord no less. Two hours down and two hours back, trapped in a car with his warm, space-consuming, citrus-scented, heartless presence. Oh, man, but she wasn't being paid enough.

Literally.

* * *

Across town, Charles stood in front of his living room window watching the snowflakes blow about in the dark. A deer. Talk about bad luck. Only in New England would a deer cause a car accident. There was a reason you didn't see Deer Crossing signs in downtown Los Angeles.

Sipping his martini, it dawned on him how lucky he was not to be hurt beyond a few sore muscles and bruises. Luckier still he didn't hit something larger, like a moose.

Maybe his good fortune explained why the fatigue and tension he'd expected to feel at the end of such a long day never fully materialized. In fact, he felt remarkably... Licking the gin from his lips, he tried and failed to come up with a word. Certainly not relaxed; he hadn't been relaxed since childhood. Best definition he had was less tense. He was less tense.

And cold, he thought with a scowl. The mile-high penthouse ceilings did little to seal in warmth. Tearing himself away from the view—there wasn't much to see anyway—he stepped down into the pit area that took up much of his living room floor space. The gas fireplace didn't throw a ton of warmth, but it was better than nothing as he settled back against the leather sectional.

He'd been warm enough in Elizabeth's car, he thought, staring at the flames. Exceedingly warm actually. Her long, lean frame gave off a great deal of heat. He smiled recalling how, while driving, the gap of her wool coat fell open, offering him a glimpse of leg every time she raised her foot to brake. He'd always known she had long legs. Barefoot, the woman was an inch off his six feet, but he'd never appreciated how shapely they were until this afternoon when every brake light forced her skirt to creep up her thigh. For the first time in his life, he found himself not minding stop-and-go traffic.

He was a little disappointed Elizabeth hadn't shown more of her edge during their drive, the spark only igniting toward the end. Having witnessed it twice in one day, he found himself curious to see how steely that backbone would get when pushed. Then again, there was always tomorrow's drive to Concord.

Recalling the look on her face when he dropped that bombshell made him chuckle. Talk about utter disbelief. Then and there, any possible bad mood he had was erased by her wide brown eyes. Granted, making her drive when he could contact a rental car agency was heavy-handed but he couldn't help himself. Especially when she was so perturbed by the notion. Damned if he knew why, but he found sparring with his secretary incredibly entertaining.

Absentmindedly, he ran his hand across his sore cheek, mirroring Elizabeth's touch in the car. Normally he had no need for idle conversation, preferring to keep his relationships compartmentalized into one of two categories: business or personal and certainly never both together. But Elizabeth intrigued him. There seemed to be a number of layers to her he hadn't noticed before. Like the fact she had a son. Made him wonder what else lay beneath her lengthy surface.

After all, it wasn't as if he was interested in a romantic liaison with her. He was merely looking to make his stay in New Hampshire as palatable as possible while it lasted.

At last, a hint of warmth began spreading its way through his body. Stretching his legs, Charles drained the last of his martini and savored the sensation. Yes, he thought with a smile, tomorrow had potential to be very intriguing.

He couldn't wait.

CHAPTER THREE

PART of Liz hoped to wake up and discover Charles's "request" to drive him had been a big misunderstanding. The other part hoped the storm reversed its sea-bound track and returned, leaving the entire state snowbound. Both parts woke up disappointed. The sky was gray but storm free when she pulled back the curtains to check. Unable to go back to sleep, Liz dressed and made her way to the kitchen only to find Andrew uncharacteristically awake and cooking frozen waffles.

"You're up early," she remarked. "There a problem?" Andrew never voluntarily dragged himself out of bed before two or three hits of the snooze button.

"Yeah, the furnace. It made too much noise."

Indeed. Liz had listened to the wheezes and grumbles all night long herself. That they were hearing the noises more often and for longer didn't bode well.

"Least you don't have to worry about being late." Grateful she couldn't see this morning's eye roll, she flipped the switch on the coffee-maker

"You're wearing that to work?" she heard Andrew ask as she was reaching for her coffee mug.

Liz glanced down at her lime-green fleece and jeans. "It's casual Friday. What about you? You wearing that?" Though he was freshly showered, he wore sleep pants and no shirt. At the sight of her string bean's broadening shoulders, Liz felt a mixture of pride and anxiety. He was growing up fast.

Too fast.

"I didn't want to get food on my shirt." While talking, he slathered both waffles with peanut butter and jelly, then slapped them together like a sandwich. "Coach's got this thing about us looking clean at pep rallies." He took a bite. "You're coming tonight, right?"

"Of course." She'd missed no more than a handful of games since Pee Wee Hockey. Making sure Andrew had someone in the stands to cheer him on was a promise she'd made long ago. "I'll be there as soon as I drop off the boss."

"You really have to be his driver?"

"For today, yes. He has an important meeting in Concord."

"What a tool."

Tool was one word for him, thought Liz chewing the inside of her cheek. Although tools didn't usually provoke sympathy with the way they spoke. She was still trying to understand her unexpected reaction last night. Matter of fact, she was trying to understand the entire conversation. What did he care about what employees—or she—thought? "Regardless, he's also my boss. I don't have much choice. I'd like to stay on his good side."

"Then I'd definitely change the shirt."

"What's wrong with my shirt? I told you, today's casual Friday."

"Casual, Mom, not ugly."

All right, so it wasn't her best look. She didn't choose the outfit to be stylish anyway. While technically Fridays were casual dress days, most of the company dropped the practice after Ron's death. With Charles always dressed so formally, wearing jeans felt out of place. She was embracing the tradition today to prove a point. A passive aggressive way of saying "you're not the boss of me, even though you are" gesture. "I don't think it's that bad," she lied.

"If you say so, but don't expect me to acknowledge you at the game if you're still wearing it."

"You have to, wise guy. I'm your driver, too."

"I'll find another." Smirking, he polished off the last of his waffle sandwich in one bite. "I better get dressed. Vic's picking me up early. Sammy's going to show us how to do the calculus assignment before homeroom."

"Wait a sec!" She reached out and caught his arm as he passed by. "I thought you and Victoria did your homework together last night." Their heads had certainly been smushed close enough over their books.

"We did, but neither of us understood it."

"So why aren't you going to see Mr. Rueben? I thought he hosted help sessions in the mornings."

"Mr. Rueben hates me."

"Andrew—"

"Come on, Mom! He's awful. He talks in

this monotone and I can't understand anything he's saying. Sam explains things better."

"Make sure he actually explains and doesn't do the homework for you." Liz had her misgivings. There seemed to be a lot of complaints about Mr. Rueben lately.

"Don't worry, I promise." He unhooked himself from her grasp and headed upstairs. "Oh, and Mom? The shirt's not that bad."

"Thanks." But as soon as she caught her reflection in the microwave, Liz knew her son was lying. The only flattering thing she could say about the lime-green fleece was that it did a nice job of bringing out her circles. Otherwise, the garment hung on her like a bright colored sack.

Liz sighed. Once upon a time she'd had potential. Tall and gawky, but attractive. Now she just looked tired. No one would look twice in her direction. Which was fine, really. After all, she had Andrew to raise now. She wasn't looking to attract or impress anybody. Besides, hadn't she dressed to impress yesterday? Look how well that turned out.

In the end, however, Liz changed. Or rather, she changed her sweater to a green and blue reindeer sweater and blue turtleneck. There was passive aggressive; then there was out and out foolish, and as much as she wanted to rebel, she also wanted to maintain some sense of professionalism. At least that was the story she sold herself. Her putting on a more flattering sweater or deciding to wear leather boots instead of quilted snow boots had everything to do with looking her best for work.

She arrived at Charles's complex five minutes to seven to find him already waiting in the doorway. Soon as she caught sight of his cashmere coat, her pulse picked up its pace. He looked, as always, amazing. It wasn't fair.

"Good morning, Elizabeth," he greeted upon opening the door.

Liz struggled to find her voice. Didn't help that he appeared to be slowly scanning the length of her while he spoke. "Good morning."

"Exercising casual Friday, I see."

"Is that a problem?"

She couldn't tell if the emotion crossing his features was disappointment or amusement or mixture of both. "Not really," he replied, shrugging off his coat to reveal an ash-gray suit perfectly cut to his broad shoulders and narrow hips that immediately made Liz glad she opted against the green fleece. "We're going to be in the car a good chunk of the day. Might as well do what you need to be comfortable."

"Well, if that's the case, would you mind if we grab a cup of coffee before getting on the highway? My first cup didn't quite cut the mustard and I could use a second." Not to mention, it would give her something to focus on besides the well-dressed man beside her.

The aftereffects of yesterday's accident showed as Charles settled stiffly into the passenger seat. Liz turned, intent on asking about his back and neck, only to forget how closely they were sitting. When he buckled his seat belt, the angle brought his face within inches. Not for the first time, Liz noticed how he gave the illusion of being far larger than he actually was. Even though she had a couple inches on him in the high heel boots, next to him, she felt strangely petite and delicate. She let her eyes travel to his cheek. Overnight, the reddened patch had darkened so it looked more like a scrape.

"Your cheek looks better."

Soon as she made the remark, the strangest expression filled his features. A bizarre combination of amazement and gratitude, as if she'd asked about something far more important than his cheek, it set off an equally strange fluttering feeling in Liz's chest. She looked to his eyes only to have him break away by settling back against the seat.

"If you want your coffee, you should get going," he said, eyes locking on the view beyond the windshield. "Otherwise, you won't have time."

They ended up stopping at the doughnut store near the exit. One of the few places Charles thought actually knew how to brew a halfway decent cup of coffee and even that was more serviceable than anything. The utter lack of decent beverages in the area was highly unacceptable, as far as he was concerned. If he was going to be stuck here awhile, he was going to have to rectify the situation. *If.* He chuckled to himself. As if sticking around would ever be an option. Better he light a fire under his lawyers.

He had to chuckle, too, at his secretary.

Casual Friday, huh? Why didn't he quite buy that explanation?

Maybe because she hadn't worn jeans to work since he'd taken over the company? More likely, this was payback for his drafting her as a chauffeur. Looked like his secretary had a little control streak along with her backbone. He would miss the skirt, or rather the view that came with the skirt. Although, he thought stealing a peek, those jeans and leather boots weren't exactly hard to look at.

What did bother him, however, was his reaction when she asked about his cheek. It was a simple enough question, one any polite person would ask. And yet, when she mentioned it, his insides grew jumbled. He couldn't remember the last time someone wondered about his well-being, least not genuinely. He didn't know what to say. So he said nothing.

"Problem?" Elizabeth's question pulled him from his thoughts. Looking up, he saw concern etched on her profile. "You're frowning," she said.

Again, caught off guard by her observation, he lied. "Coffee's weak. I prefer a stronger brew."

"You are very picky about your coffee."

The understatement made him chuckle. "You've noticed, have you?"

"Hard to miss the personal coffeemaker set up in your office."

"Good point. What can I say? I have high standards."

"Must make life difficult," she replied.

"How so?"

She shrugged. "What do you do when things aren't up to snuff?"

"Then I don't waste my time. Why bother settling for second best?" He went to sip his coffee only to decide to follow his own advice and set the cup in the holder. "I learned a long time ago that what you get in this world is up to you." God knows, no one else gave a damn.

"True."

The edge to her tone caught his attention. Sounded like he'd touched a nerve. What hard lessons had life taught her? he wondered. Whatever they were, the scars didn't show on her face. Her profile was clear and youthful, lacking any of the ravages life could heap upon a person. Then again, as he well knew, scars didn't always show, either.

What were her scars?

Curious, he adjusted in his seat so he could view her better. As he learned yesterday, her face was remarkably readable, her thoughts and emotions playing out quite visibly. A horrendous trait in business, but utterly fascinating and refreshing to see. "How long have you worked for Bishop Paper?"

"Why do you want to know?"

Case in point. Mistrust colored every feature. "Curiosity," he replied. "We're going to spend the day together. Seems like a good time to get to know my assistant better."

"No offense, but I've been working for you for weeks. You never showed interest before."

That's because he hadn't realized how interesting she could be till now. "We've never had two solid hours with nothing to do but talk before."

"Suppose not."

And she sounded so thrilled to be in that position now, Charles thought with a smile. Obviously he was going to have to pull answers out of her. "So," he began again, "how long have you worked for Bishop?"

"Eighteen years in April."

"That long? You must have started young."

She frowned, as though he said something wrong. "Young enough."

"Do you like it?"

"I'd like to keep my job, if that's what you're asking."

"Don't worry, your head's not on the chopping block." At least not during his short tenure. Hopefully Xinhua management would be smart enough to keep her as well. "Were you always my father's secretary?"

"No, I started as a file clerk. Your father promoted me about ten years ago, when Peggy Flockhart retired."

Peggy. He remembered the name. *You spend more time with Peggy than you do your own wife.* "Were you two—" he cleared his throat of the sudden frog that lodged in it "—close?"

"With Peggy?"

"With my father?"

Elizabeth touched the brakes. "What exactly are you asking?"

"You said yourself my father considered you all family. I'm simply curious how close."

"Not as close as you're implying, that's for certain."

Her answer was sharp-edged, and jabbed

him in the gut. "Then how would you describe your relationship?"

"We were friendly. He was pleasant to work for. Made me—made everyone at the company—feel like we were helping him achieve something."

"It was all about the company then."

"It was about being part of the company," she replied. "There's a difference."

"Maybe," he replied. "Maybe not." Charles hadn't realized till she answered that he'd been looking to see whether somewhere along the line Ron found something—or someone—better. But he hadn't. In the end, it still amounted to his father putting the company first. Guess the lawyer was wrong. The old man hadn't changed.

He'd studied the cars in the next lane. Elizabeth was a confident driver, he noticed. She navigated the highway traffic with admirable ease. Although she'd been outraged at the suggestion, he wouldn't have blamed his father if he'd dallied with his assistant. She was definitely dalliance-worthy, if one were so inclined.

In the next seat, Elizabeth let out a long, frustrated-sounding sigh. "I enjoyed working for your father," she continued, explaining her comment further. "He made me feel…" She shrugged. "Appreciated."

"As opposed to me?" Charles asked.

"I didn't say that."

She didn't have to; the implication was obvious. "I assure you, Elizabeth, I appreciate your services very much."

"Of course you do," she replied, her smile closer to a smirk.

"You sound skeptical."

"Really?" She maneuvered the car into the next lane. "Whatever gave you that idea?"

"You don't believe I appreciate you?"

"What I think is that appreciating a person and appreciating their services are two very different things."

Charles sat back. "I get it. This is about my turning down your request for a raise. I already told you—"

"I know—" she cut him off "—you can't make exceptions."

"Precisely."

"And you're simply trying to cut costs. Nothing personal."

Again, correct. And yet hearing his words spit back at him rankled. Made him feel like he was the villain when he was simply practicing sound business.

Charles shifted in his seat. Since when did he care what employees thought of him anyway? He wasn't here to court favor or win friends. He was here to sell a company. So why then, did he have this inexplicable urge to argue his point till Elizabeth agreed with his logic?

Why, all of a sudden, did one secretary's negative opinion sit so uncomfortably in the pit of his stomach?

CHAPTER FOUR

"You barely touched your lunch."

They stood in the coatroom of a local restaurant after having said their goodbyes to several key business leaders and the governor. "Was there a problem with your order?" Charles asked, his voice sounding attractively deep.

Liz ignored the way his breath tickled her ear as he held her jacket. He was lucky she couldn't dump the lettuce in his lap. When he insisted on her driving him today, she assumed that was all she'd be doing. She hadn't expected to be dragged into the meeting or to a fancy restaurant where even the waiters were dressed better than her.

"My salad was fine," she replied, shrugging the jacket out of his grasp.

"You certain? Because you could have ordered something different."

"I said it was fine. I simply wasn't hungry." Feeling self-conscious tended to kill her appetite. Everyone staring in their direction as they walked through the dining room.

All right, maybe they weren't staring just at her. They could have been staring at the governor. Or Charles. He looked as out of place as her, only for the opposite reason. Even next to the state political leaders, he broadcast a genetic superiority over everyone else in the room. He didn't need the cashmere overcoat and expensive Italian shoes for people to know in a battle of the strongest, he would always come out the victor. If she weren't so annoyed with him, the female side of her would be flooded with appreciation.

But she was annoyed, so she stomped ahead of him out of the restaurant, moving fast enough that he had to jog to catch up.

Took him about a block. But he did. To her irritation, he wasn't even out of breath from the exertion.

"Are we in a rush to get someplace?" he asked.

"Home," she snapped. "If that's all right with you." On top of everything else today, the meeting and lunch had run long. At midafternoon, it was already starting to get dark. The streetlamps and headlights were on, and people had hit the streets, trying to beat the weekend traffic rush but in reality, causing one. The roads north would be jammed with cars from Massachusetts and south heading to ski country, Andrew's hockey game faced off in a couple hours, too. Dang.

"You could have given me a heads-up," she said. "Let me know that you expected me to join you in those meetings."

"I thought that was understood. After all, you have the best grasp of Bishop's green policies."

Bull. "Until yesterday, you planned to attend alone."

"Yes, but I didn't, so why not take advantage of the resources available? The governor, by the way, looked very impressed."

"Sure he was. Right after he got over the fact I was wearing a reindeer sweater."

"You were the one recognizing casual Friday." He wore an amused smirk. So help her, if she didn't enjoy receiving a paycheck she'd smack him. "Besides," he continued, "didn't you attend meetings like this when you accompanied my father?"

"No. Ron was the people person. He didn't really need anyone's assistance."

"What a surprise."

"Excuse me?"

Charles's comment said he hadn't realized he'd spoken aloud. He had, though, and there was enough edge in his muttered words to make Liz forget she was supposed to be angry. "You said you weren't surprised."

"Are you?"

"No, I suppose not. Ron was always considered a bit of a maverick. So are you," she noted.

"Hardly" was his terse reply.

"That's not what the business magazines say."

"The business magazines exaggerate."

"How so?" She was curious. Understanding how he ticked might hold some clues to what the future held for her and the rest of the company.

"Well, for one thing, the term maverick implies recklessness. I do not believe in being brash. I prefer to base my decisions on economics and good fiscal sense, not my gut."

"You're saying your father didn't?"

"I have no idea what drove my father's

decision-making, although it's clear looking at the numbers, it wasn't economics."

"Told you, he considered us family."

Charles's reply was a derisive snort.

They'd reached the parking garage lobby. As if on command, the elevator door opened the moment he pushed the button and Liz found herself ushered into the small steel space. The air smelled faintly of body wash. How did he do it? she wondered. How'd he manage to fill every room, every space he entered with his essence, dwarfing all around him? Needing space, she stepped to her left and leaned against the wall.

"You don't put much stock in sentimentality, do you?"

"I put stock in numbers," he replied. "Pluses, minuses, profits, losses. Those are things you can see and measure. Not some vague-sounding concept pulled out of thin air."

Like promises. Pretty words that didn't mean a hill of beans. Liz understood what Charles meant. Lord knows she wished she didn't, but she understood all too well. "Why put stock in something that will only fail you?" she agreed in a soft voice.

"Exactly," he replied, eyes meeting hers. A kind of sympathetic surprise shone in their blue depths. "All sentiment does is cloud your judgment. Better to avoid emotion altogether."

Such attitude didn't bode well for Bishop Paper, did it?

"You're right," she said. "You're not like your father at all."

"Told you."

Liz wasn't sure what to say. Instinct and experience told her to detest the man. Bishop Paper—or rather the fate of the company— meant nothing to him beyond the numbers on a balance sheet. And yet at the same time, something about the way he spoke held her back. His cavalier tone sounded too forced; his defense of the bottom line too emphatic. A part of her couldn't help feeling almost... sympathetic. Could it be, Charles's icy nature didn't run as deep as everyone thought?

Her suspicions grew when, as they reached their floor and the elevator doors slid closed behind them, Charles reached out and grabbed her elbow. "Hey!" His gentle grip stopped her immediately.

Turning, she found him firmly planted in

her personal space, once more giving the illusion of being larger than everything else around him. "For what it's worth," he said, his blue eyes finding hers, "you did fine back at the meeting. It was good you were there."

She told herself the free-fall sensation his compliment sparked was her imagination.

Liz had been right about the traffic. This year's abundant snowfall made for terrific skiing. A boon for New Hampshire's economy, but bad for anyone driving the highway on a Friday afternoon. Particularly once it got dark. With each press of the brake light, Liz could feel the time inching closer to six-thirty. Drat. She was going to miss the opening face-off.

Next to her, Charles shifted in his seat, his frustrated sigh echoing her thoughts. Part of them anyway. She doubted very much he suffered from the internal confusion that had plagued her since leaving the parking garage. In the dark confines of her car, it was impossible to shake Charles's closeness. Every movement, every breath reminded her nerves he sat a slip of an arm away. Strangely enough, her elbow was still warm where he touched her, too. Odd that the touch of a man who prided himself on his cool detachment could radiate such heat.

At last, a sign announced their exit was only a few miles away. "About time," Charles said. "This traffic has been outrageous."

"Happens when you take too long to get out of the city," she replied. "Given how snowy it's been, we're lucky the traffic isn't worse."

"I'd hate to see how."

So would she, to be honest. She glanced at the dashboard clock. Six twenty-seven. By the time she got off the highway, took Charles back to his condominium, then drove out to the rink in Franklin she'd be lucky if she caught more than the final period. And that was if Charles didn't insist on stopping by the office first.

"What's the problem?" Charles asked.

"What makes you think there's a problem?"

"Well, the sigh you let out a second ago for starters. Plus you keep tapping the steering wheel and making little frustrated noises in the back of your throat. Do you have plans that you're late for?"

Why did that question sound probing? "Face-off," she replied. "Puck drops at six-thirty."

"Hockey?"

"Uh-uh. My son's high school team is playing their biggest rival tonight."

"And you're planning to attend. On a Friday night."

"Of course." As if she'd make any other choice. Andrew was her son. "I attend as many home games as I can."

"Interesting."

"I don't know if it's that. In fact, if you ask Andrew, he'll tell you my presence is unnecessary."

"Why do you go, then?"

"Because. As his parent, I know he might not care right now, but when he looks back, he'll remember I was there."

"And be saved the sting looking up and discovering you weren't."

A full feeling stretched across Liz's chest. Yes, she thought, that was it exactly.

The traffic in front of her slowed to a stop. Terrific. In the back of her mind, Liz quickly calculated time and distance. Gilmore was fifteen minutes off the exit. It was another fifteen or twenty to Charles's complex, ten more to Franklin....

Screw it. She told Andrew she'd be at this

game, and she wasn't about to renege, at least not because her boss made her play chauffeur. Besides, it served Charles right after making her attend those meetings today.

They inched their way up to the exit ramp. Stopping at the top, Liz took a moment to read the sign indicating Gilmore was to the right, before turning left, toward Franklin.

They arrived in Franklin shortly after the start of the second period.

"Let me get this straight," Charles said as they entered the lobby of the Franklin rink. "Your son plays for the Gilmore High School hockey team and you have to attend his home game two towns away. Why is that exactly?"

"The rink got struck by lightning last summer and caught fire. Coffee?"

"Good Lord, no." Charles scowled at the hot beverage vending machine in the ice rink lobby. "That's not coffee. It's lukewarm brown water."

"Suit yourself." She tapped her foot waiting for her hot cocoa to finish. "It gets cold near the ice."

"I'll survive. Trust me." He scowled again, his distaste obvious. "I'll definitely survive."

Liz imagined he would. Just as she imagined she was going to pay for this forced detour. Although Charles outwardly appeared calm, she wasn't fool enough to believe the façade for one second. After all, he'd appeared agreeable regarding her casual day rebellion this morning and look how that turned out. She wound up sitting in a meeting full of state leaders looking like a teenager in a reindeer sweater and faded jeans.

"Why doesn't Gilmore fix the rink?" he asked, his lips curling into a frown as he peeled his loafer from a patch of soda-encrusted rubber flooring.

A quick look at the scoreboard told her the game was still scoreless. Good, she hadn't missed much.

"The town plans to as soon as it appropriates the funds," she told him. "Until then, however, we're out of luck."

"You don't say."

She ignored the sarcasm. Part of the reason the town lacked funds was that they'd hoped to secure help from Ron Bishop, but he'd died before the request could be finalized.

No sooner did they enter the arena than the nudges and curious stares began passing from person to person. In her haste to make the game, she'd forgotten one-third of the team had parents who worked for Bishop Paper. Maybe this wasn't such a good idea after all.

With the burn of what felt like a hundred stares frying her skin, she pointed at a section of bleachers to the left of center ice. "I usually sit a few rows from the top," she told him.

"Looks cozy."

Liz was about to retort when it dawned on her his remark might be more than sarcasm. He had, after all, been in a car accident yesterday. "The top row would allow you to lean against the wall, if that would be more comfortable."

"Why would you...?" He looked taken aback.

"I didn't know how your back and neck felt after yesterday."

"Oh, right. Wherever you normally sit works fine." Confusion continued lining his face. Finally he seemed to recover, the lines smoothing and his face lighting with an expression she couldn't define. "Thank you for asking."

"You're welcome." His confusion trans-

ferred itself to her. It was a simple question.
No reason for him to look at her so strangely.
Or for butterflies to skitter across her stom-
ach.

The crowd parted for them like the Red
Sea. Liz suppressed the urge to hide her face
as she climbed the bleachers. So she had arrived at the game with Charles Bishop. Big
deal. Charles was the one who should feel out
of place.

Except *he* was used to being scrutinized.
He mounted the bleachers with the same im-
perial bearing he always had, nodding hello
to employees and acting as if it was perfectly
normal for him to be there.

To Liz's dismay, the crowd surged back
as they sat down, forcing them to crowd together on the bench seat. Charles's leg ended
up pressed against hers, the pressure stretching from hip to knee. Liz gripped her cocoa,
thinking the liquid's temperature cold in com-
parison to the temperature spreading across
her leg. What was that she said about it being
cold near the ice?

"How are they doing?" she asked the
mother sitting next to her. Might as well try

to look unaffected. "I noticed no one's scored yet. Have there been many shots on goal?"

"A ton, but nothing's breaking our way," the woman replied.

"Sooner or later one will go in."

Just then, the Gilmore goalie made an amazing save, causing the crowd to erupt. Forgetting her self-consciousness, Liz cheered, too. It wasn't until she finished that she noticed Charles studying the ice with discernible confusion.

"Not a hockey fan, I take it?" she asked.

"Wouldn't know," he replied. "This is the first game I've ever watched. Which skater is your son?"

"Number thirty-two. The tall one. He's a right wing on the first line."

"First line?"

Oh, this was going to be interesting. "There are three lines of offense. They rotate in and out to keep from getting too winded. Andrew's on the first line. There he is now." She pointed as Andrew leaped over the wall and back onto the ice.

"Hey, Lizzie!" someone two rows down called over. "Did you see the coach from Trenton's here?"

"He is?" Scanning the crowd, she finally spotted the man by the Gilmore coaches' box.

"Any word about Andrew?"

"Not yet." Inside, the question made her wince. She hadn't wanted the subject brought up in front of Charles.

As she expected, he picked up on the reference right away. "Trenton Academy? You're thinking of sending your son there?"

She could imagine his number-oriented mind mentally recalculating her salary as he spoke.

"The coach is recruiting him," she replied. "But nothing's carved in stone."

"Interesting" was all he replied.

Out on the ice, Andrew received a pass. He brought the puck down the ice and at the last minute, passed to the center, who took a hard slapshot. A disappointed groan ripped through the crowd as the goalie made the save.

"Keep the pressure on, Sean!" a man hollered from the front of the bleachers.

Charles frowned. "Was that Van Hancock?"

"Uh-huh. His youngest son, Sean, plays center. The kid's only a sophomore, but he's having a terrific season." She winced as a player checked Andrew into the boards in a fight for the puck. As always, her heart waited until Andrew skated safely away before leaving her throat.

"Not a big fan of the hits, I see," Charles noted.

"I know checking's part of the game, but when it's your child getting nailed, it's hard to remember that. Once, when Andrew was really small, and believe it or not there was a time not so long ago, I yelled at the referee for not calling a penalty." Her cheeks grew warm remembering. "I was told to sit as far back in the bleachers as possible from then on."

"By the official?"

"By Andrew. He still says I have the loudest voice in the rink."

"At least you're here and cheering," Charles replied.

As if she would make any other choice. Andrew was her son. "I make it a point to attend as many games as I can. Work doesn't always make it possible."

"Does his father come to the games, as well?"

Bill? "Better luck getting it to snow in July." Too late she realized how embittered she sounded and she looked to her lap. "Sorry. Andrew's father is a sore topic."

"I take it he's not an active parent."

Active? More like absent. "Let's say he's not very interested in being a father."

"I understand."

There sounded like empathy in his voice. Curious, Liz looked in his direction, her breath catching as she caught the last of a shadow ghosting across his profile. She knew that shadow. She'd seen it in Andrew's expression when he didn't know she was looking, and in her own childhood reflection. For the second time that day, unexpected sympathy stirred in her heart.

"Did you play sports in high school?" She tried her best to picture a younger, carefree version of him running around an athletic field and failed.

Which was why she wasn't surprised when he shook his head. "Didn't have time. Too busy with school."

That she could picture. "Let me guess, you were top of your class."

"Actually at seventeen I was a freshman at

Cal Tech. I opted to graduate early and take a scholarship."

Wow. "I'm impressed."

"Don't be," he said. "I had a lot of motivation."

What kind of motivation? Had he been looking to prove himself? Or prove something to his father? All of a sudden, her image of Ron Bishop as zesty and compassionate no longer seemed to line up quite as neatly as it once did.

"Funny how circumstances can fuel your resolve," she said.

"That's for sure."

Silent agreement wrapped itself around them.

For the next forty minutes, Liz found herself explaining the action on the ice. To his credit, Charles acted interested. She wasn't surprised to see him grasp the concepts quickly and by the end of the third period, he had a working knowledge of high school hockey.

As for the game itself, the score remained tied, with both goalies stopping shot after shot. Then, with a minute left to play, Andrew broke free. Once again, he brought the puck down the ice and passed off to Hancock, whose shot went wide. The puck ricocheted off the boards, and Andrew was there to pick it up.

Liz jumped to her feet along with the rest of the crowd. "Come on, buddy!" she screamed. "You can do it!"

She held her breath as Andrew's wrist shot careened toward the upper left hand corner of the goal. At the last minute, the goalie dove sideways, his arm raised upward. The puck tipped off the top of his glove and into the net. The crowd cheered wildly. Liz jumped up and down, clapping and cheering. From the corner of her eye, she saw Charles studying her. In her zeal, she'd forgotten he was there. "Andrew's right," he said. "You do have the loudest cheer in the stands." Liz's cheeks grew hot.

"Not in a bad way, though," he added.

"Thank you, I guess."

"You're welcome." He smiled and Liz felt the most uncharacteristic wave of shyness wash over her. It forced her head to duck downward and catch her lip between her teeth. Reaching up, she combed her fingers through her hair, only to discover upon looking through her lashes, that Charles was doing the same. That their actions mimicked one another only made the shyness more acute.

The buzzer sounded, breaking the exchange. Waking from her daze, Liz sat down to gather her things. Charles did the same, his hip brushing hers in the process. Quickly they both slid apart.

"How did you enjoy your first hockey game?" she asked him.

"It was passable. Your son seems like a pretty good player. Not that I'm in much of a position to judge."

"Thank you." She tucked her hair behind her ear. "And thank you for letting me come straight from the highway."

"If I recall, I didn't let you do anything. You were driving and since I don't enjoy long walks—at least not in these shoes…" To illustrate, he lifted his foot. "Anyway, you can repay my good nature by taking me to dinner."

"Dinner?" Liz repeated.

"Yes, dinner. I'm starving and I am not about to buy my dinner out of a vending machine. At least not during this lifetime. There's a restaurant in Gilmore. Nothing fancy, but I believe they serve a decent enough meal."

"You mean Mahoney's?"

"That's the place. We can stop there on the way to my complex."

Liz wasn't quite sure how to respond. Having shared one meal with the man already, she really hadn't been expecting to share a second. Worse, she wasn't expecting her stomach to grow all fluttery at the suggestion.

"I can't," she told him, surprised at how strongly she felt her regret. "I have to drive Andrew."

"Bring him along. Didn't you say he needed several meals a day?"

She did. But including Andrew didn't sound like the best idea. She hadn't been out with another man since Bill. When Andrew was younger she hadn't wanted him to feel threatened and now she didn't have the time nor energy to date.

This isn't a date, a voice reminded her.

"Unfortunately I can't," she told him again. "I have to give Andrew a ride home."

"Hey, Mom!" With impeccable timing, Andrew appeared at the rink's edge. "Vic and I are going to hang at Sam's for a little while to celebrate. She said she'd give me a ride home." His attention flickered to Charles and back. "That is, if you don't need me."

"I'm fine, sweetheart," Liz replied. "Be home by eleven."

Next to her, Charles's smile turned smug. "Will you look at that. Guess you're free to eat after all."

He offered her his arm. "Shall we?"

CHAPTER FIVE

CHARLES had driven by Mahoney's a number of times since coming to Gilmore, but never gone inside. The brick-faced restaurant with an Irish flag by the door wasn't his usual style of restaurant. He preferred a sedate atmosphere where you could hear yourself think and get business done. However, since the parking lot filled night after night, he assumed it must have something to offer.

Standing in the doorway, brushing snowflakes from his curls, he was greeted by the sounds of laughter and Irish music. A blackboard on the wall listed homemade macaroni and cheese as one of the specials and suggested patrons try this month's local microbrew, an aptly named Twelve Weeks of Winter Dark Ale. The number of customers still occupying tables after the dinner rush was over appeared to confirm his assumption.

"Apparently this is the place to be," he mused.

"It's popular." Elizabeth's reply was as stiff as her spine. She was annoyed he'd insisted they stop, but couldn't say anything, having dragged him to a high school game.

As he examined the rustic decor, Charles realized the situation was the opposite of today's lunch, this time with him the fish out of water. Except after a lifetime of being the outsider, the role no longer bothered him.

Looking back, the entire day had been a game of one-upmanship, hadn't it? Of course he didn't *need* her to attend his meeting with the governor—although her impressive knowledge of Bishop's research was useful—he'd simply wanted to see how she'd react. Her feistiness was fun to watch. And, if he were to be completely honest, part of him wanted to reassert his authority. It bothered him how much her approval seemed to matter. Like now. He shouldn't care about how annoyed she was; her job was to do as he asked. And yet, the frown on her face ate at him like a bad case of heartburn.

"No need to look like you're on the way to

prison," he said. "Surely having dinner with me isn't so horrible, is it?"

"Let's just get a table." Unaware of his study, she sighed and combed the hair away from her face. The way the dark strands moved through her fingers reminded Charles of cascading brown satin. Did she have any idea how much attention the gesture drew to her? Or how many heads turned upon her entrance into a room? Heads that would turn regardless of who accompanied her. Mentally he shook his head. And she'd been concerned about looking out of place during today's meeting. Even in an out-of-date sweater and stony expression she presented one stunning sight. He was pretty sure the governor was smitten the minute he met her.

Gently he guided her by the elbow to a table near the bar. He'd been doing a lot of that today, touching her. Normally he avoided casual physical contact, particularly in business settings, preferring to reserve touching for meetings of a more intimate nature. But, like so many other instances today, Elizabeth had him deviating from the standard.

No sooner were they seated than a waitress came by, dropped a pair of menus on the table and promised to return shortly. Charles questioned that as he watched the woman disappear across the room. "So," he said, shrugging out of his coat, "is this where you hang out on Friday nights?"

"No" was her short reply.

"You mean there's a second town hot spot?"

"I mean I don't hang out in bars on Friday nights," she said, burying her head in the menu.

"Here I thought that uncomfortable look was all my doing."

"Don't assume it's not."

"Funny." He hooked his arm over the back of his chair. "You were fine with my company at the hockey game."

"That was different. You were already in the car and I didn't want to miss my son's game."

The picture of her proud smiling face popped into Charles's mind. He'd spent almost as much time watching her cheer on her child as he had the game. Her son was a lucky kid. What did it feel like to be the recipient of such sincere attention? To have someone who actually wanted you around. Who enjoyed your existence.

Returning his attention to the woman across from him, he shook off the hollow feeling threatening to break loose in his chest. "And now, evil boss that I am, I pay you back by buying you dinner."

"No, you're buying yourself dinner. I'm here because I had to drive you."

"You're eating as well. Should I ask for separate checks?"

She drew the menu closer. "If you want."

"Spoken like a real trouper." Behind his menu, Charles hid a grin. His good humor had returned. He'd been right to insist on her company. "I don't want. What I do want, however, is a drink. Think the bartender makes a proper martini?"

"I'm sure he knows how to mix drinks."

"Mix, sure. Anyone can mix gin and vermouth. It takes an artist to make a martini."

That made her set down the menu. "I didn't know bartending was an art."

"All drinks require skill to make them, if you want to drink something decent."

To his pleasure, he could see her fighting a smile. "That's right. You're a drink snob."

"To which I make no apologies." All the talk about drinks had made him impatient, and he signaled for the waitress. "Now, why don't you hang out here on Friday nights."

"I don't hang out anywhere. I have a child, remember."

"He's in high school, though. I didn't think they needed babysitters at that age."

"Are you kidding? High school is when they need the most supervision. Surely you remember."

"All too well."

"So do I." Though she tried to sound non-chalant, she failed. Her voice was too regretful, her eyes a tad too evasive.

"Did something happen?" he had to ask.

He watched as she played with the edge of her menu, her downcast lashes casting half-moon shadows on her cheeks. "Andrew happened."

"Oh." *Oh.* Now he understood. "You're afraid Andrew and his girlfriend will…" Rather than say the word, he arched his brow.

"He's seventeen and in love. You know what that's like. You tend to believe forever is really possible."

A pipe dream if ever Charles heard one, though something about the way Elizabeth said it cut him to the quick. Earlier, she did

say her ex was an absent father. He had a suspicion that bastard did far more.

"For what it's worth," he said, "not every
teenager tries to have sex. And if he does,
the odds of the same fate happening twice
are fairly slim."

"In other words, I should relax because sta-
tistics tell me to."

"No, you should relax because your boss
told you to."

"Oh, well in that case…"

The waitress appeared to take their order.
Elizabeth ordered both specials. After a moment's contemplation, Charles did the same.

"What happened to the martini?" she asked
him when they were alone again.

"I decided to play it safe. Odds are the
items are featured because they're popular.
Plus," he teased, "you ordered the same thing,
so if it's unacceptable, I can blame you."

She laughed. Having never heard her do
so, at least not in close proximity, he had no
idea how pretty a sound her laugh could be.
Or how pretty she looked when doing so.
The corners of her eyes crinkled and two
tiny dimples dented her cheeks. That he was
responsible gave him a warm, satisfied feel-

ing. "You should laugh more often," he said. "Looks good on you." So did the blush creeping into her cheeks.

"I laugh," she replied, playing with her fork.

"Not at work." Correction, not in the office. In *his* office.

"Crack a few more jokes and I might."

"That your way of saying I'm too serious?"

"I'm not sure serious is the word I'd use."

The waitress returned with their drinks. At the sight of thick foam floating atop dark brown liquid, Charles attempted to suppress his grimace. Across the table, Elizabeth coughed, a sign his attempt failed. "Let me guess," she said, "you know beer about as well as you know hockey."

"I was underage in college, remember." He took a sip. Just as he suspected. Heavy and bitter. Sort of like how he felt thinking about his past.

"What word would you use?" he asked, returning to the earlier conversation. "Or are you too much of a lady?"

He liked the smirk she tossed at him. "Scary. People are afraid of you, you know."

"I know." He paused. "You're not, though."

"No, I'm not. Not anymore."

"What changed?"

Leaning forward, she cupped her chin in her hand, causing the neon bar lights to cast red highlights on the crown of her head. "To tell you the truth, I don't know."

Their eyes connected and Charles saw the flash of approval he'd been seeking all day. The sight struck him hard, arousing more than his body. He hadn't expected the sensation to be so compelling. All of a sudden he found himself seeing details in his companion he'd never noticed before. Like the crook at the bridge of her long nose, and the lines at the edge of her eyes that spoke of experience and smiles. The delicate curve of her lips. He imagined curves of a different type beneath her reindeer sweater. He must have been blind these past few months.

The corners of his mouth curled around his beer glass. "Well, whatever the reason, I'm glad."

Unless his girlfriend was hiding in the comforter wrapped around his shoulders, Andrew was home alone watching television when Liz walked through the door. "Thought you and

Vic would be with your friends celebrating," she said. "And what's with the blanket."

"I'm cold, and Vic's got SAT class in the morning so she dropped me off early. How was your 'date'?"

"That wasn't my date. I told you, I had to drive Mr. Bishop today, remember?"

"I didn't know you were taking him to my game."

"Had to. We were running late and if I'd taken him home, I'd have missed your game-winning goal." She tossed a pillow in his direction, which he neatly ducked. "He was impressed, by the way."

"Must have been since he took you out to dinner."

"He was hungry. Really, Andrew, the man's my boss."

"So?"

So, she didn't appreciate the inference. "This was a one-time deal." Come Monday morning, everything would return to normal. Except she wouldn't be afraid of him anymore, she thought smiling to herself.

From his perch on the sofa, Andrew was giving her a look. "Did you get something to eat?" she asked him.

"Made grilled cheese when I got home."

"I'm guessing you left the dirty pan on the burner, too, hoping I'd wash it for you?"

The teenager gave her an exaggerated grin, mimicking a three-year-old in an attempt to look cute. Another night she would have told him to get off his duff and wash his own pan, but tonight she didn't feel like arguing.

"Oh, hey, Mr. Rueben wants you to call him next week," Andrew called out as she walked toward the kitchen.

"Did he say why?" Though the calculus teacher wanting to speak with her couldn't be a good thing.

"Nope. Just to call."

Intuition told her Andrew was holding back, but like the dishes, she decided to let the subject drop. It was late, and she was in too good a mood to press him for information.

She hated to admit it, but Charles made a pretty good dinner companion. Handsome, charming. More than once she'd found herself laughing. He'd told her she looked good when she laughed, she thought with a rush of heat. Been a long time since a man told her she looked good period. She'd almost forgotten what it felt like to have someone look at her as more than Andrew's mother. To be seen as a woman.

Will you listen to yourself? Now she was the one acting like tonight had been a date. As if that were possible. A man like Charles, rich, gorgeous...uninterested. He'd said so himself—he liked the best. She was pretty certain that standard applied to more than coffee and cocktails, same as she was certain a thirty-four-year-old secretary with a GED and teenage son didn't fit the bill.

Still... She turned on the faucet and grabbed a dish sponge. Tonight had been a nice change of pace. Even if it was a one-time thing.

A one-time thing. Charles's sparkling blue eyes danced in front of her, setting off an ache, big and cavernous in the hollow of her chest, and she suddenly remembered why she'd avoided dating all these years. Because the high from the encounter never lasted. You found yourself wanting another fix. And another. Craving the rush so badly you willingly believed all the false promises you were being fed. Eventually, though, reality broke the spell, leaving you alone and pregnant with no one to depend upon but yourself. She'd done the discarded and unwanted deal seventeen years ago. She had no desire to revisit those days again. Far better to stay on the wagon.

She shivered. Andrew was right; the town house was cold. Whatever warmth had carried her home had faded. Best she put Charles Bishop out of her mind, make herself a cup of tea and go watch television with her son. Where she belonged.

The next morning, the town house was still cold. Liz stared at the automatic thermostat sending a silent message for the temperature to increase at a faster rate.

"The water's not real hot, either," Andrew said from behind her.

"I know." Her own shower had been lukewarm at best, and only that temperature for a couple minutes.

"The furnace was making those weird noises again last night."

"I know that, too. Sorry," she quickly added, pinching the bridge of her nose. It wasn't Andrew's fault the furnace was acting up. Or that she was cold and hadn't slept well. All night long her king-size bed, normally her weekend sanctuary, had felt too big, the unused portion of the sheets too cold. "I'll turn up the thermostat. Maybe the house will warm up while we're out."

"Hope so. Cold showers suck."

"Thank you, Captain Obvious. Go get dressed. I promised your coach you'd be there to help set up tables."

She walked back to her bedroom kicking herself for not setting up the coffeemaker the night before. It was way to early on a Saturday morning to be up without a decent cup of coffee.

A decent cup. That's what Charles would call it, she realized with a shiver. So much for putting him out of her mind. She hadn't been awake a half hour and already he'd crossed her thoughts. Irritated even more, she grabbed her blow dryer. Maybe a rush of hot air would clear her head.

"Mom!"

Liz dropped her chin to her chest. If she got to dry her hair.

"Hey, Mom!"

"Check the kitchen counter," she hollered back. Whatever it was he was looking for, she was sure it would be there. She was beginning to think he never actually looked for anything in the first place.

Flicking the hair dryer on, she tipped her head upside down and started drying. The hot hair on her scalp only served to remind her how cold the rest of her body was. The church hall better have working heat, she thought to herself.

There was a knock on the door and Andrew's half dressed torso appeared. "You've got company," he said in a tight voice.

Company? "What are you talking about?" Must be one of the other hockey parents. And here she was still in her bathrobe with wet hair.

"And put a shirt on. It's too cold to be wandering around without one. Hey, where are you going?"

"To put a shirt on. You told me to."

"After you… Never mind." Teenagers. Tightening her belt, she headed downstairs. Three steps from the bottom, she almost tripped in shock.

"What are you…?" She was too surprised to finish the question.

Charles stood in her living room looking

like a GQ model in a supple black leather jacket and faded jeans. He was peeling an equally supple pair of gloves from his fingers. When he saw her, he smiled. "Good morning to you, too."

A blush shot straight to her toes. "Sorry," she said, brushing the wet hair from her face. "When Andrew said someone was here to see me, I wasn't expecting you."

"Obviously."

Dear Lord, but he looked amazing. Better than he had in her dreams.

The thought struck her sharply as she realized he had indeed been in her dreams. No wonder she couldn't shake him from her head this morning. "What are you doing here?"

"My smartphone," he replied. "I think I left it on your dashboard last night."

Of course. Why else would he come to her home except to retrieve something? "I'll go unlock my car and see."

"No need. If you give me your keys, I'll look myself. You're not really prepared for heading outside."

Liz looked down at the faded terry-cloth garment that barely skimmed her knees. In spite of her having pulled the belt as tight as possible, the front still gapped around her legs, revealing part of her thighs. She gave the belt another tug only to look up and find Charles's eyes watching her with cerulean intensity. All of a sudden the room halved in size. "Guess not," she managed to choke out.

"Not that the robe's a bad look. A little more casual than the reindeer sweater, but..."

Feeling her skin growing warmer, she turned away from his grin.

"And you give me a hard time for answering the door without a shirt on." Andrew ambled down the stairs, heavy-footed in his bare feet. "No one needs to see that robe."

"Manners, Andrew."

"Sorry," he replied, catching her tone.

"This is my son, Andrew," she said. "Andrew, this is my boss, Charles Bishop. Charles thinks he left his phone in my car."

Andrew tossed a head nod in Charles's direction; a greeting Charles, much to Liz's surprise, tossed right back. "Congratulations on the game last night."

"Thanks. Mom, we got to get going. I told Coach I'd be there at quarter to."

He was reminding her? That was different. "Andrew's team is hosting a pancake breakfast at the Episcopal Church this morning to raise money for the rink," she told him.

"Right, the new roof. I won't keep you then. Just let me know where you keep your car keys and I'll be on my way."

"Sure. I keep them on the kitchen count…" Halfway across the room a thought struck her, causing her to turn. "How'd you get here anyway?"

"Rental car. The agency dropped one off late last night."

"So you won't need my chauffeuring services anymore."

"No, you are no longer at the mercy of my schedule."

Lucky her, she thought as her fingers closed around the key ring. No more forced dinners.

An awkward silence settled between them. Liz looked down at the keys. Seemed silly to chase him off when he'd driven across town so early in the morning. The man probably hadn't even had his decent coffee yet. And, the fundraiser could use all the attendees it could muster. "If you haven't had breakfast yet, you're welcome to join us."

"You're inviting me to the pancake breakfast?"

Silly, she knew. He probably had a dozen other, better things to do. For that matter so did she. "If you're interested. Most of your employees will be there at one time or another."

"So attending would be good public relations."

"You could say that."

Charles stroked his jaw. As he thought, his eyes took on a strange, almost grateful expression. "Sounds like a good idea. I think I will join you."

In spite of herself, Liz's pulse skittered. "Great," she replied. "Let me finish getting ready and we'll go together."

Behind her, she heard Andrew march upstairs and loudly shut his bedroom door. "Don't mind him," she said. "He's mad he didn't get a hot shower. Our furnace is being temperamental."

"I see."

Yet again, they fell silent. Liz toed the carpeting with her bare foot, trying to think of something to do besides smile mutely. "I should get dressed, too," she said finally. "Do you mind waiting?"

"Not at all. I'll stay down here and warm

up from the outside." To illustrate, he rubbed his hands together and blew on his fingers. "Maybe your furnace will start working better while I wait. Your son's right—it is chilly in here."

That's funny, Liz thought as she trotted back upstairs. Soon as Charles walked in the house, the cold hadn't bothered her at all.

CHAPTER SIX

"YOUR mother tells me you're thinking of
going to Trenton Academy next year."

"Uh-huh."

"Good school."

"Yup."

This, thought Liz, was a mistake. Her son
had been sullen and monosyllabic all morning.

"Trenton hockey plays in a bigger division
than Gilmore High," she explained, setting
her plastic fork down on her foam plate. "If
Andrew goes, he'll have to repeat his junior
year, but he'll also be seen by a lot more colleges, and have a much better shot at a scholarship to a Division I school."

"Impressive. You must be excited."

Andrew shrugged.

Oh, yeah, definitely having a refresher
course in manners later.

In spite of the early hour, the tables in the basement of St. Mark's were full, mostly with families of team members. The players themselves milled about refilling the buffet pans with trays and pouring orange juice into plastic drink cups. The cool basement air smelled of bacon and maple syrup.

With a slight hint of citrus body wash. Liz wasn't sure she could truly smell Charles or if her imagination was teasing her senses, but each time he leaned back in his metal folding chair, she swore the aroma drifted past her. How could one man smell so good? Or look so good this early in the morning? Even after putting on makeup and her best turtleneck sweater Liz was pretty sure she still looked tired. Charles on the other hand, looked like he stepped out of a magazine.

And then there was Andrew. She could see this behavior if he was younger and Charles was a potential boyfriend, but neither could be further from reality.

"Of course, he has to keep his grades up to qualify. To play varsity sports, you need to maintain a C or better."

"Which I am," Andrew said, more to his pancakes to anything else.

"So far," she told him. "We haven't seen this semester's progress report yet." That reminded her; she needed to call Mr. Rueben on Monday. Hopefully it wasn't bad news. "He's doing great except for calculus. Math's always been a bad subject. Neither of us know what we're doing in it."

"Mom gave up freshman year when they started geometry."

"Excuse me for not remembering the Quadratic Equation."

"AX squared plus BX plus C equals zero."

Both she and Andrew looked up at Charles, who shrugged. "The Quadratic Equation." Out of the corner of her eye she caught Andrew's barely concealed eye roll.

"Anyway," she said, shooting her son a look, "Andrew decided to take advanced calculus instead of the easier level so this year's been a challenge. So far so good, though."

"That's terrific," Charles replied. "Better to take on the challenge than sit back and rest easy, right?"

"I agree." Annoyance forgotten, she smiled proudly at her boy. For all his sulky insolence this morning, he was a good, hard-working kid.

A tap on her shoulder pulled her out of her thoughts. Peeking over her shoulder she saw Leanne in her blue and gold Boosters' Club fleece. "Can I borrow you for a minute?" she asked Liz after saying hello to Charles.

"Well…" Both Andrew and Charles had taken their phones out and were actively ignoring one another. "Sure. What's up? Is there a problem with the pancakes?" Liz asked, knowing full well as soon as the older woman took her arm and dragged her toward the buffet line what this meeting was really about.

"What on earth is Mr. Bishop doing here?" Leanne asked.

"Having breakfast like everyone else in the room."

"With you and Andrew? What's going on? Van told me the two of you were at the hockey game together, and you went to Mahoney's afterward." Her dark red lips formed a large O. "He didn't…"

"What? No! Don't be ridiculous." What other wild rumors were out there? "He came by this morning to get his phone—which he left in the car," she added before her friend could comment, "and I told him about the breakfast. He thought it might be a good idea to mingle with his employees."

"He's only mingling with one."

"He's eating," Liz repeated. "What's the man supposed to do, travel from table to table with a foam plate in his hand mooching bacon?"

Back at the table, Charles and Andrew were still ignoring one another. As if sensing her scrutiny, Charles gave a quick nod in her direction. He then pointed to her empty coffee cup and gestured if she wanted more. Smiling, Liz shook her head.

The exchange didn't go unnoticed. "Are you sure you two aren't...?" Leanne waggled her eyebrows.

"No. No way." The happy, full feeling she had a moment earlier faded away, replaced by a hollowness in the middle of her chest. "He's our boss, Leanne. He wouldn't be interested in me in a million years."

Briefly she relayed the whole story, about Charles's accident to her driving him all day and how they ended up going straight to Andrew's game. "If I'd brought him home first,

I would have missed everything, so I dragged him with me. Afterward, he wanted to get something to eat so we stopped on the way back. There's nothing else to it."

"And here I thought you'd crossed over to the dark side. Although to be honest—" the woman leaned forward "—I'm not sure I'd blame you if you did. Mr. Bishop might be a coldhearted bastard, but he's a gorgeous cold-hearted bastard."

"He's not a bastard, period." Liz surprised herself with how easily the defense tripped off her tongue. "In fact, if you talk with him, you find he's an okay guy. Interesting actually. Did you know he went to Cal Tech when he was seventeen?"

"Was this before or after he cut Ron out of his life?"

She didn't know how to answer. A week ago, a day even, she'd have readily agreed with the cutting comment. "I'm not sure the business with Ron is so cut-and-dried. Something tells me there's two sides to the story, and that maybe Ron's wasn't so innocent."

"I take it back…you have gone to the dark side."

"That's my point. I don't think Charles is as big an enemy as we made him out to be." Leanne would think so, too, if she'd heard the injured resignation in Charles's voice every time the subject of his father came up.

"Who's not the enemy? Bishop?" Van asked. He ambled toward the group, Doug Metcalf trailing a step behind. Wherever there was gossip, the pair was never far. "Morning, Lizzie. How was your night?" Innuendo dripped from his words.

Liz returned his smirk with a scowl of her own. "I don't know, Van, you tell me since you're so busy telling everyone my business."

The salesman threw up his hands. "Sorry. Didn't mean to touch a nerve."

"Well, you did." She refused to be fodder for watercooler gossip, especially when there was no realistic chance that what they were gossiping about could ever happen. She glared at all three of them before turning on her heel and marching away.

Charles sat alone when she arrived at their table, absently playing with his empty juice glass. Andrew had moved to the next table to talk with Victoria and her friend. When he saw her, he instantly straightened. "Problem?"

"Only that the office grapevine has been working overtime. Leanne wanted the details about our 'date.'"

Brow furrowing, he resumed fiddling with his cup. It was obvious the news didn't sit well with him. "What did you tell them?"

"The truth." Bitter as it sounded out loud. "I'm not sure they believed me, though."

"Why not?"

"Because I told them you weren't as big a bastard as everyone thought."

"Did you, now?" He sat back, arms folded across his chest and flashed her a smile. Liz felt her skin blush.

"Don't get too cocky," she told him. "They didn't believe that, either."

"No one ever does. I think, in fact, you're the first. Thank you."

His smile shifted and his expression grew serious. The sincerity in his voice traveled to her chest, settling directly over her heart.

"You're welcome," she said, and wondered if the ache she felt was hers or his. The pancake breakfast faded away, leaving them the only two people in the room. Like this morning, she felt the distance between them halve. And for a crazy second Liz caught herself wishing the rumors were true.

Charles broke the spell first. "I have to go," he said, although he made no effort to move. "I have a conference call with my attorney about a deal I'm working on. Would you like me to walk you to your car? I'll treat you to a real cup of coffee on the way."

"Thanks, but I promised I'd stay and help the committee clean up. Besides, I've got Andrew. He needs new work boots."

"Then I guess I'll see you Monday."

"At work." She added the words as much for herself as anything. Charles's deal comment reminded her exactly who the man sitting next to her was. A man far removed from Gilmore, Bishop Paper and everything else she could name, including her. A man who didn't believe in anything but balance sheets and figures. A man who, soon as he could, would leave for his next big deal. A man she had no business letting get under her skin.

First a high school hockey game, then a pancake breakfast. What next, running for town council? That'll be the day, Charles thought with a shake of his head. What would happen next was finalizing his deal with Xinhua, so he could rid himself of this company and get on with his life.

Alone in his office while he waited for his overseas call, Charles perched on his desk and stared at the White Mountains. He never realized how picturesque they truly were. Their snow-covered slopes glistened under the cloudless winter sky. If he squinted, he could make out tiny dots moving along their surface. Skiers. Good day for skiing, he imagined—if you were into the sport.

Did Elizabeth ski? Be a shame to risk breaking one of those long legs. Bet she ice skated, though. Charles could easily see her guiding her son around the rink when the boy was younger. Catching him when he fell. She'd be smiling the whole time, too. A real smile. Not one reserved for public viewing.

Come on, Charles, get yourself together. His lack of focus these past sixteen hours astounded him. His mind insisted on wandering all over the place. In fact the only consistent thoughts in his head were about his secretary. Seemed like every five minutes her name would pop into his head or he'd get an image of her.

Like the way she looked this morning in that terry-cloth robe. Demure looking and yet the neckline spread open just enough he could tell she wasn't wearing anything underneath. The memory caused a sudden tightness in his body.

This was ridiculous. He'd had attractive secretaries before. Why did this one woman have him feeling so distracted and out of balance? He should be focused on the upcoming negotiations and how soon he'd be rid of this company. Wouldn't be long and he could finally close the book on his father, his childhood and every other bad memory for good.

On his desk, his phone vibrated, rattling loudly against the wood. Charles waited two rings before answering. "*Ni hao ma*, Mr. Huang. I've been expecting your call."

"All I'm saying is it wouldn't hurt for you to show the man a little courtesy. He is my boss," Liz said as she pulled into her driveway.

"I know. You've only told me six times since we got in the car."

"Maybe because I want to make sure you get the message." She looked over at the figure slumped in the passenger seat. Her refresher course started when she pulled out of St. Mark's parking lot, and as it progressed Andrew had sunk lower and lower in his seat till he sat with his knees wedged against the dashboard and his cheekbone resting on one fist. "What is wrong with you anyway?" she asked. "You've been surly since last night."

"Nothing."

Intuition said otherwise so she pressed. "You sure?"

"Don't worry about it."

Code for he wasn't going to share until he was ready. "Sorry, but I'm always going to worry. Comes with the job."

"You done?"

"For now."

She stepped out of the car and promptly shivered. Without a fan blowing hot air on her feet, the sunshine wasn't nearly as enjoyable. Thankfully she remembered to turn up the thermostat before leaving. With luck the town house was finally warm and toasty.

"I thought you thought Mr. Bishop was a

tool," Andrew said as she fiddled with the door lock.

"I was wrong. Happens you know."

"So you like him."

Liz paused. Was that what his mood was all about? Because Charles joined them for breakfast? "Sweetheart, you know that Mr. Bishop only joined us because he wanted to mingle with his employees. Build up goodwill and all."

"He didn't mingle with anyone but you."

True, but she wasn't going to read anything into the attention. No doubt Charles had his reasons. He wasn't a man who did anything without a reason.

Andrew pushed open the front door and they stepped inside. It was like stepping into an icebox. "Is it me, or is it colder than when we left?" Liz asked.

"Colder," Andrew replied. "Definitely colder."

Frowning, Liz knelt down and put her fingers to the baseboard heat. Given the temperature she programmed into the downstairs thermostat, hot air should have been coming out the vent. But the vent, along with the entire baseboard for that matter, was cold.

The morning's pancakes turned to lead in her stomach. This wasn't good.

By midafternoon she learned exactly how bad the situation she had on her hands was.

"I can fix it so you have heat," the plumber told her, "but bottom line is the furnace needs to be replaced."

Liz had known this day would come eventually. "How much?"

When he told her, her heart stuck in her throat. No way could she swing the amount. She was going to have to take a bigger home equity loan. If she had more equity to borrow against, that is after she budgeted for Trenton. Real estate prices in town weren't what they used to be.

Telling the plumber to go ahead and order the furnace and make the repair, she wrapped herself in a blanket and waited to warm up. Her stomach and her head hurt.

"Everything all right, Mom?" Andrew stood on the stairway wrapped in his comforter.

"Fine, sweetheart. The plumber says we're going to need a new furnace."

"Do we have the money?"

The stress must show on her face because he always asked when they were faced with a big expense. Charles was right; she did have a lousy poker face. "Don't worry about it," she told him, aware of how ironic the comment sounded coming from her.

"Because I don't have to go to Trenton or I can get a part-time job…"

"Don't be ridiculous. Furnaces break. It's a cost of homeownership. Why don't you text Sammy and see if you can hang out at his place for the rest of the afternoon? By the time you get back the furnace should be working."

"Okay."

She waited until he went back upstairs before laying her head on the armrest. Times like these the longing she kept buried in her heart rose up like a monster. A chenille throw was no substitute for a pair of strong arms and a shoulder to cry on. It wasn't that she couldn't handle problems on her own. She could and had since high school. But oh, to have someone to hold her close and tell her they'll take care of everything—even if the words were a lie… Sure would be nice.

She closed her eyes and imagined her throw was the aroma of citrus body wash.

Apparently headaches came in threes. Andrew failed his last two calculus exams. That's what Mr. Rueben wanted to talk about. "I'll work with him as much as I can, but I think he'd benefit from more intense one-on-one help as well," the teacher told her. "Someone who will sit with him a few hours a week and help with homework. He's lacking a number of basic skills he'll need to progress next year."

As well as succeed at Trenton, thought Liz.

Of course doing well at Trenton wouldn't matter if he couldn't play hockey, and unless he got his grades up, hockey wouldn't be in Andrew's future much longer.

Liz thanked the teacher and hung up, wondering where she would find a good tutor. Andrew would suggest his friend Sammy, but as good a student Sammy was, Andrew needed more. He needed an adult who would make sure he focused on his work. Later this morning she'd call the guidance office and ask for a few names. Right after she made an appointment with the loan officer at the bank. She was going to have to push up the loan process to pay for her new furnace. Which she had to arrange delivery for.

No wonder she still had her headache from Saturday. With a sigh, she lay her head on her desk. She knew something was up with Andrew's math grade. He was always making comments about the homework. Why didn't she press for more information?

The longing to be held struck again, stronger than ever.

"Need an aspirin?"

Lifting her head, she saw Charles watching her from the doorway of his office. He wore his standard work uniform, shirtsleeves and loose tie, but it wasn't his casual sex appeal that made her breath catch. It was his expression. He wore a look of concern that, focused on her, felt a lot like a hug.

"I came out to learn where you were on the notes from Friday's meetings and saw you had your head down on your desk," he explained. "Figured you had a headache."

"Headaches, plural," she corrected. "Unfortunately I don't think aspirin will help."

"What happened?"

"Nothing I can't handle." She sat up straighter and combed the hair from her eyes. "You said you were looking for something? My notes?"

"The notes can wait. Tell me what's wrong."

"I told you, it's nothing."

"Elizabeth." Squatting so that he was eye level, he grabbed both arms of her chair and turned her until they were face-to-face. "When are you going to accept the fact you aren't a very good liar? The fact you're upset is written all over your face. Did something happen with Andrew?"

Liz studied the man in front of her, amazed at the concern she saw in his eyes. "I—" She didn't know what to say. The very idea he offered to listen…it was a first for her. She wasn't used to having people offering support. Usually they ran the other way. The longing that had been twisting in her chest since Saturday suddenly exploded. She'd been handling everything on her own for so long now…

Before she realized, she was blinking away moisture from her eyes.

"Hey— Hey…" Charles moved closer, bringing his comforting warmth into her space. "It's okay. Is it Andrew?"

"I'm sorry," she said, dabbing at her eyes. "I'm being emotional for no reason. It's silly really."

"Why not let me be the judge of that," he said, his voice soft and gentle. "Tell me what's wrong."

Liz sniffed. "Where should I start? With the fact my furnace died and I have to take out a loan to pay for a new one? Which I'm already doing because I need to pay private school tuition…"

"Wait. I thought Andrew was recruited to play hockey for them."

"In a roundabout way. The school doesn't give out sports scholarships, and Andrew's grades don't qualify him for much in the way of academic merit money. We qualify for some breaks based on need, but it's not enough to cover everything. Though all of that won't matter if the kid can't pass math."

"He's not?"

"Spoke to his teacher about five minutes ago. He needs a tutor. Oh, and did I mention the kid told me this morning he needed new shoes and skates? Turns out he grew since last

fall. Chances are he needs all new pants, too."
She forced a wan smile. "Aren't you glad you
asked?"

"You definitely have a few things on your
plate."

"Fortunately I'm used to a full plate by
now. As long as nothing else major breaks or
Andrew gets himself in trouble, I'll be fine."
Pain had settled behind her eyes, probably
from sniffing back tears. She pinched the
bridge of her nose. "Maybe I will take those
aspirin," she said, reaching for the drawer.

"Here, let me." He reached across her to the
top drawer where she kept a spare bottle of
pain relievers. Flipping off the top, he shook
two capsules into her palm, then handed her
the coffee cup by her keyboard. Liz watched
everything with mute appreciation.

"You're welcome," Charles replied, reading her mind. He sat back on his haunches
watching as she swallowed the pills. "Thurs-
day, when you asked for the raise. Was that
to pay for Trenton?"

"Sort of." She nodded. "I figured the extra
money would help cover the loan payments."

"And I turned you down."

"I knew going in there was a good chance

you would." Amazingly she felt the need to reassure him.

"But you asked anyway."

"Go big or go home, right?" Charles frowned so she explained. "It's something Andrew and his teammates say. Meaning go all out."

"Live or die trying, you mean."

"Exactly."

"A motto I always believed myself." He looked to his knees, but not before Liz caught an uncharacteristic look of regret. "I'm sorry," he said. "I didn't know what you needed the money for."

"Would it have made a difference?"

He didn't answer, because they both knew it wouldn't have. Charles lived by numbers, not emotion; he said so himself.

Yet, here he was listening to her complain. Go figure. "Now that I hear myself, I sound pretty whiny. I should be grateful for what I have instead of complaining. I mean, figuring out how to pay for private school is hardly a life or death situation."

"You want the best for your son. Nothing wrong with wanting the best, remember?"

His remark forced her mouth to curve upward. "You would believe that," she replied. "Andrew did without so much growing up. No father, no grandparents, and I want him to have all the opportunities and choices I missed on. It's that sometimes it feels like I'm swimming upstream to do so."

Nodding with understanding, Charles asked, "What if you had the raise?"

"What do you mean?" She tensed, refusing to listen to any implication in his words. No way she would be lulled into getting her hope up a second time.

"I mean, you can have the raise. I'll put in the paperwork this afternoon."

This couldn't be real. Charles Bishop did not just reverse his decision and give her a raise. Things like that did not happen. "Wha—what about not making exceptions?"

"I decided one time wouldn't hurt. I admire what you're trying to do with Andrew. Besides—" he pushed himself to his feet "—I look at it as an investment. Having a potential NHL star indebted to me could come in handy someday."

"I don't know what to say." Her heart was stuck in her throat along with a lump the size of Franconia Notch. Together they choked off her ability to do much more than smile and blink back a fresh round of tears.

"You don't have to say anything. You would have gotten the raise at your performance review anyway. You do earn your paycheck."

"Thank you." Her shoulders felt like they'd had a ten ton weight taken off them. "Now I really have to make sure Andrew passes math."

"That's right. He's failing calculus."

"Hanging on by a thread. I have to call the high school and get a list of teachers who tutor. Of course, Andrew will no doubt complain about each one. When he's backed into a corner, he gets disagreeable."

"Wonder where that comes from?" Charles asked, with a smile that made Liz want to stick her tongue out. Certainly lightened the moment.

Only a moment, though. She sighed as her frustration rose again. "I blame myself for some of the problem. The way he complained about the class and his homework, I should have realized he was having trouble sooner. But he kept telling me he was going over the homework with Sammy."

"You need to cut yourself a little slack. You're doing the best you can."

"Thanks. Want to come by and tell Andrew that for me when he starts barking about his tutor?"

"I've got a better idea. How about I tutor?"

What? Her mouth dropped open. "You?"

"Sure. Last time I checked, I was pretty good with numbers. Cal Tech, remember? And, he won't be able to say I'm one of those 'boring old teachers.'"

True enough. But why? Why was he suddenly doing so much to help her when two days ago, he barely cared she existed? It didn't make sense.

"Because I want to," he replied when she asked him. He caught her chin between his thumb and forefinger, forcing her gaze upward until she met his eyes. Searching their depths, she looked for signs of motive only to see nothing but deep blue. Suspicion warred with gratitude.

As if sensing her hesitancy, he fanned his thumb across the curve of her chin. "Because I want to."

It was only after he closed his office door that Charles realized he'd never retrieved Elizabeth's notes. He'd get them later. His head was still spinning over what he just did. Had he really offered to tutor her son? And spontaneously reversed his decision on her raise? Because she'd told him her problems?

Yes, he realized with a twisted feeling, he had. Listening to her explain why Andrew going to Trenton meant so much to her, the choked off emotion quivering in her voice, cut him deep. Here was this woman trying so hard to be both mother and father. She wasn't forgetting Andrew existed or shunting him aside in favor of another, more important pursuit. She was trying to give her son the world. And he impeded her efforts.

Would it have made a difference? Soon as she said those words, and he'd looked into her shining hazelnut eyes, he felt three inches tall. For the first time in his life he regretted a sound business decision. All of a sudden he wanted nothing more than to make up for his decision and prove to her he was more than some profit-minded boss. All because the sheen in her eyes kicked him so hard his chest ached. He wanted those eyes to smile at him, goddammit, not look teary-eyed and sad.

Letting out a long breath, he washed his

hand across his face and tried to regain focus. Negotiations with Xinhua were going well. Mr. Huang Bin liked what he'd seen so far. Meanwhile, Bishop Paper appeared to be bucking the trend as far as paper companies in New England. Last quarter reports showed profits up by three percent. Whatever flaws his father had as a parent, he knew how to run a company. Bishop Paper was in far more solid fiscal shape than he would have believed. And if the company implemented the greening initiatives they discussed Friday, like switching to hydropower, they would be in a strong position for the future.

Not that you'll be here to see, he reminded himself. Hydropower and chemical-free bleaching were items for Huang Bin to decide. He would be long gone by then.

For some reason the thought didn't give him as big a thrill as it usually did.

Must be he was tired. Too many late nights reviewing reports were catching up with him. Then again, what else was there to do around here besides work? Or hockey games and pancake breakfasts...

Dropping into his chair, he swiveled around to the window, marveling yet again at the beauty of his view. He had made Elizabeth's day with his spontaneity, he thought with a smile.

That, he realized, gave him a far bigger thrill than negotiations.

CHAPTER SEVEN

"ANDREW, turn off the video games and get your math book out."

"To do what? Mr. Bishop's not even here yet. What am I supposed to do, stare at the problems I don't know how to do?"

"How about looking like you're trying?" she shot back.

Liz looked at the clock. Charles would be here any minute. The imminent arrival gave her barely enough time to straighten up. Her son could at least contribute by not sprawling across the sofa. "And put your empty soda can in the recycling while you're at it," she added, nudging his left leg.

"Now," she added when the teen didn't move.

"All right, all right. Stop freaking out."

"I am not freaking out. Charles was nice enough to offer his help."

"Charles?"

She shot her son a glare. "The least we can do is make sure the apartment isn't a pigsty when he arrives. Straighten out the couch pillows. And refold the afghan."

"Good thing you're not freaking out," Andrew muttered.

Maybe she was freaking out a little. It wasn't like Charles hadn't been here before. But yesterday's visit had been unexpected.

So was tonight's when she thought about it. Today's turn of events still had her head spinning. One minute she had the weight of the world pressing down on her shoulders, next Charles was giving her a raise and offering to tutor her kid. Like her very own Prince Charming.

Why? She figured the raise happened because he felt guilty. Having one's secretary break down could gnaw at your conscience. But tutoring Andrew? He claimed he offered because he wanted to, and she was trying very hard to take him at his word, something her experience made very hard to do. How many promises had Bill made and broken?

Promise me you'll love me forever?

Baby, you know I will.

This wasn't the same. Charles wasn't promising to love her. He wasn't even promising to stick around. He simply offered to help her son with his math homework. Maybe a guilty conscience was at play here, too. After all, he made both offers at the same time.

The doorbell rang. Liz jumped. Darn it, right on time. Nervously she glanced around the living room. Had the red sectional always looked so ratty? And that blue throw draped over the back. Could the room look more mismatched? She could only imagine what Charles thought. Probably ranked her decor right up with Mahoney's, the ice skating rink and the local coffee. Below his standards and lifestyle.

"You look a million miles away."

She jumped again. Charles stood behind her, shrugging off his overcoat. A coat that, she realized, was more expensive and luxurious than any of the furniture.

"Everything all right?" he asked.

"Everything's fine," she lied. *Giving myself a dose of reality, is all.* "I didn't hear you come in, is all."

"A voice hollered for me to let myself in."

Must have been Andrew. "We're still working on his manners."

"No worries," he said, draping his coat over the back of the sofa. "I'll get my revenge soon enough."

He'd come straight from the office because he still wore his charcoal suit and silk tie and as usual looked amazing. Sleek, sexy and yet—she realized with a quiver—strangely comfortable looking amid the worn furnishings.

"I told Andrew to set up at the table so you'll have plenty of room to work," she said, pointing to the butcher block table that doubled as a dining room and office. Andrew stood at the head chair rooting around his backpack.

"Hey, Mom, do you know where I put—"

"Front hall near the shoes. We're working on memory, too," she added.

"I heard that!"

"You were meant to," she shot back.

She and Charles shared a smile. The man might not offer smiles often, at least not unguarded ones, but when he did, the results could make your knees weak. Liz had to grab the back of the sofa. "I can't tell you how much I appreciate your helping him."

"I gathered as much from the five times you thanked me at work today." His smile turned warmer and for a second, he looked about to say something more. He didn't, though.

Instead, loosening his tie, he called over to Andrew, "What are we tackling tonight, anyhow?"

"First order derivatives." Andrew, who was in the process of crossing the room with his newly discovered math book, rolled his eyes. "Can't wait."

"Andrew!"

Charles laughed. Deep and rich and full, a sound made for turning insides into mush. "I'll change his mind."

Yeah, good luck with that, thought Liz. She had a feeling nothing would change her son's mind—about math or anything else for that matter.

Thankfully the "pep" talk she and Andrew had earlier about making an effort sunk in. Amazing what the threat of losing hockey could do for motivation because the kid actually paid attention to what Charles had to say. What's more, he was doing the work. After five or ten minutes of discomfort, the two of them managed to put their heads together. They were currently cruising through Andrew's homework assignment.

"Then you take the exponent, multiply by the front number, and subtract one from the exponent."

"That's it?"

"That's it. The key is not to memorize the equation, but to focus about the steps you need to get there. Your problem is you're trying to skip steps and that won't work. Math is all about breaking down big pieces of information into smaller pieces. The trick is not to try to do everything in your head or you get confused."

"I've been telling him that since he was eight," Liz remarked from her position at the kitchen counter.

"Mom!"

"What, a mother can't gloat when she's right?"

From over Andrew's bent head Charles flashed a grin in her direction that shot straight to her knees. It felt different having a man in the house. Back when she was a teenager, this is what she imagined happy homes were like, parents and children spending time together, sharing each others' lives. No step-father with roaming eyes or mother complaining about having one too many mouths to feed. Tonight reminded her of the normalcy she'd strove to give Andrew his entire life. With a father figure to explain homework and a husband to lean on when times got tough. An old-fashioned and outdated fantasy? Sure, but what good was a fantasy if you couldn't create a perfect one, right?

Shaking off the rush of longing, she returned to chopping carrots. In the other room, Andrew grunted his understanding to something Charles was saying. She resisted the urge to look to the dining room table again. Her mind was already having difficulty staying focused.

What was it lately that had her thinking about fantasies anyway? Was it Andrew getting older? Or something else? Like a pair of concerned blue eyes that had been there to listen to her problems.

Remembering the touch of Charles's fingers against her chin, she smiled.

"Mom?"

Andrew stared at her with a look of embarrassment and frustration.

"I asked when we were having dinner," he said.

"Um… Twenty minutes." Unless she faded out again and burned the chicken.

"Smells delicious," Charles said. "I'm having trouble concentrating with my stomach growling."

"You're staying?"

"Why wouldn't he?" Liz cut in. Truthfully she was as surprised as Andrew. Sure, inviting a man to come by at dinnertime implied staying for dinner, but she'd assumed he wouldn't want to. "I'm afraid we're only having roast chicken breast and vegetables."

"Anything you serve sounds terrific as long as it's homemade. I haven't had a decently cooked meal in ages."

He hadn't? "You don't have someone to cook for you?"

"My housekeeper isn't what I'd call the best cook. She has an unhealthy fascination with ground beef."

"I have the feeling you'll be saying the same thing about me. When it comes to cooking, I'm all about the basics." Thank goodness she decided to take chicken out this morning instead of hamburger for meat loaf.

"I'm sure it'll be fine. Something tells me I'll enjoy anything you make."

He's being polite. Even so, her stomach did a somersault. "Just for that," she told him, "you get to have wine with dinner."

Not to mention that if he planned on joining them for dinner, she would need a drink or two herself.

Dinner was delicious. Granted, he wouldn't call the meal five-star cuisine. But sitting with Elizabeth and her son, sipping an okay glass of wine and listening to them talk about their days, Charles decided it was the best chicken he'd had in a long time. He told her as much after they finished and Andrew had retreated to his room.

Flashing a half smile, she pushed herself from the table. "It's all right, Andrew's out of earshot," she said, gathering the plates. "You can stop being polite."

That she couldn't take him for his word stung. "You don't believe me?"

"The man who called the chef at Mahoney's a philistine? No."

"Mahoney's is a different story."

"Oh, really, how so?"

She was heading into the kitchen so he grabbed some plates and followed. "The person who makes that concoction you called macaroni and cheese Friday night does not qualify to be called a chef. And besides, the chef at Mahoney's isn't…" *Isn't you.* The thought stopped him in his tracks.

Elizabeth glanced at him from over her shoulder. "The chef at Mahoney's isn't what?"

"Isn't going to make me do dishes," he lied. She'd never believe the true answer. He was having trouble believing he had the thought himself.

Didn't matter. His lie earned him one of those laughs he enjoyed hearing. "If you think that'll get you out of the chore, you're wrong."

"What about Andrew. Does he get the fun of helping, too?"

"Normally, yes, but I think I need a break. I'm sorry he's being so sullen."

"I didn't think he was being so bad."

"Let me guess, you were worse."

"I plead the fifth."

That earned him another laugh and Charles

decided he'd scrub dishes all night so he could keep hearing the sound.

"He's really a pretty helpful kid. And friendly. I don't know what's going on with him these days."

"Maybe he's got girl problems or something."

"Nope. He and Victoria are still thick as thieves."

She turned to take the stack of plates from his hands and their fingertips brushed across each other. The contact, brief as it was, sent a surge of heat down inside him. She felt a reaction, too. If the color flushing her cheeks didn't say so, her barely audible gasp did.

"Wash or dry?" She moved to the sink, turning her back to him and her voice took on a higher pitch. "Since you're a novice, maybe you should stick to the easier of the two tasks and grab the dish towel. You can dry the pots and pans when I get to them."

"All right." What he truly wanted was to reach out and touch her again, to determine whether the spark was a one-time anomaly, but the skittishness in her voice warned him away.

He watched as she scraped the plates into

the wastebasket, muttering some comment about a lack of a garbage disposal, before stacking them in the dishwasher. Then she turned on the faucet. Steam and apple-scented bubbles began to rise up from the stainless steel.

By now, the silence hanging between them had grown thick and awkward, the lightheartedness from dinner vanquished by one accidental brush of their hands.

"Do you and Andrew eat dinner together every night?" he finally asked, trying to draw the moment back.

"As often as possible." Elizabeth plunged the saucepan into the suds and began swabbing the inside with a sponge. "I sort of insist. With me working, nights and weekends are the only family time we have. Although nowadays, between hockey and school and *Victoria*, we don't have as many meals together as we used to."

"I could count the number of meals my mother and I ate together on one finger," Charles replied. "I defined the term latchkey kid."

"Your mother worked?"

"Hardly." He reached for the pan she'd finished rinsing only to be disappointed when her fingers avoided his. "On second thought, maybe she did. Lord knows she put a lot of effort into keeping her boyfriends happy." Including ignoring her child. Charles had always believed if not for the child support Ron begrudgingly sent, she'd have checked out without him. "At any rate, I became very adept at reading a room service menu at a young age."

"Explains your obsession with high quality food." The comment was lighthearted, but there was empathy shimmering in her soft brown eyes. The way the emotion wormed through him took him by surprise. He hadn't expected to feel so…so *comforted*.

"I spent the better part of my childhood avoiding dinner with my family," she said as she submerged another pot. "Wasn't too hard. My mom was more interested in my stepfather and her new family. Most of the time I would make myself a sandwich and eat it in Bill's car."

She offered a wry smile. "In retrospect, spending time in the backseat of a car probably wasn't the best plan. But I was a teenager and in love."

And believed forever was possible. Wasn't that what she said the other night? He tried to reconcile a young, love-struck Elizabeth sneaking off to be with her boyfriend with the woman standing next to him. He couldn't.

"Your family must be proud of how you're raising Andrew," he remarked, trying to bring her back to more positive subjects. When she got sad, the sparkle left her eyes, and he didn't like the look.

Unfortunately he picked a bad topic for instead of brightening, she grew a little sadder. "They've never met him. I left home when I was pregnant and that was it."

"Then they aren't in Gilmore."

"No, a few towns south," she answered. "I followed Bill up here. He had a job lined up in Franklin. Then when our relationship fell through, I stayed."

"And Bill?" He suspected he already knew the answer.

"He didn't. He's in Florida now."

Charles wanted to strangle them all. How could they let her slip from their lives so easily? Then again, hadn't he asked the same question of his own parents?

They were a lot alike, weren't they? Left

to fend for themselves, only she'd had it far, far tougher. His admiration for her grew.

"At least you can pride yourself on saying everything turned out well in the end," he said. "Raising Andrew on your own that is."

"I didn't have much choice once he was born. Don't get me wrong," she added hastily, finishing another pan and rinsing it under the water. "I love Andrew with all my heart..."

He interrupted the needless apology. "No need to explain. I understand."

"Thanks."

"You're welcome. For what it's worth, if I'd had a Bill with a car to eat in, I would have chosen that route, too. Well, maybe not exactly with a Bill, but maybe a Betsy or a Betty..."

His voice drifted off as their hands touched again. This time the spark burned stronger. Charles slid his fingers forward, letting their length align with hers, their slick, soap-covered skin caressing.

A small breath cut through the thickened air. Elizabeth was studying their hands with hooded eyes, her breath coming in ever shortening bursts. For a moment, neither of them moved. Charles's pulse raced. He felt like he stood on the edge of a great unknown not sure if he should step or not. This sensation, this heat, this whatever—he didn't know what word to use—was foreign to him.

Then, quick as it sparked, the moment shifted. "Last pan," Liz said. She pulled her hand away. "Your obligations for the evening are complete. I'll manage the rest on my own."

"You don't have to," he told her. Beneath the dishcloth, he balled his hand into a fist and wondered if he was only talking about the dishes. "I can help."

"No need. You've already done more than enough."

Though she wore a smile, it couldn't mask the hint of brittleness in her words. Where connection had been, awkwardness rushed in to take its place. "Thank you again for helping with Andrew tonight."

She was backing off. Shoving distance between them, and Charles was pretty sure he knew why. She'd felt the same spark he did, and was turning cautious, unsure about what the connection meant. He knew because he felt the same way.

"You should probably get going," she told

him. "I don't want to keep you here any longer than necessary."

"You're probably right. I have work to do." Plus, he wanted to process what happened. Figure out what he wanted to do with the attraction that was clearly flowing through him right now. At the moment the male part of him screamed for him to explore it further. He needed a step back to allow logic a say. "I'll see you in the office tomorrow."

"Thank you again for helping," she said.

Her soft smile begged to be tasted. "Please stop thanking me," he said. "I wanted to help." Then, because the male part of him couldn't help itself, he paused at the door and let his eyes drift to her pink lips. "Good night, Elizabeth."

Liz was surprised her hands weren't trembling when she locked the door. Lord knows her insides were a complete jumble of anxious energy.

You were imagining things, Liz. His eyes did not zone in on her mouth just now. Those touches meant nothing. The accidental brushing of two hands doing dishes. Her insides ached for no reason. That had to be the explanation. She'd been fantasizing about how good a pair of arms would feel around her and she started projecting. Right? *Right?*

Or was it? In her heart she knew she hadn't imagined the way his eyes darkened as he said goodbye. But why would Charles want her? Was it because he figured, with the office grapevine already gossiping, why not take advantage of the situation? Because, after hearing her pathetic story, he figured she was an easy mark?

God, but she wished she knew which scenario was true. She wished she hadn't let her thoughts drift to fantasy. She wished she could tuck the need and awareness back into hibernation where they belonged.

But most of all, she wished she knew which scenario frightened her more: that she did imagine everything or that the desire she saw in Charles's eyes was real.

"Good morning, Elizabeth."

Charles's silky voice shot straight to the base of her spine, much to Liz's dismay. She'd spent the night in her cold empty bed battling images of blue eyes and soap-slicked hands. Now, having finally gotten her thoughts somewhat under control, he unlocked them again with three simple words.

She hated him.

"Good morning," she replied, keeping her eyes on her paperwork. She might not be able to keep her body from reacting, but she could pretend it wasn't. "Doug Metcalf emailed you last month's sales figures. I printed out a copy and put the report on your desk."

"Thank you. And thank you also, again, for dinner."

"Thank you for helping Andrew and with the dishes."

She heard him chuckle. Since she still refused to look in his direction—doing so would only make her blush or give in to some other foolish reaction—she couldn't see his expression, but she could imagine the sexy twinkle in his eye. "Well, aren't we the grateful duo this morning," he said, his voice continuing to be a low, honeylike drawl. "How did you sleep?"

"Fine. The town manager's office called as well. He'd like to schedule a meeting with you for next week." She began sifting through the papers on her desk. "I told him I would get back to him with some potential dates...."

His hand reached out and stilled hers. "Are you planning to avoid eye contact all day?"

No, only till she regained a sense of reality. She stared at the hand resting on top of hers. Like so many of their physical encounters, it was hardly a touch at all. A quick pull of her hand would break all contact. Problem was she didn't want to pull away. *She wanted more.*

"I was simply reaching for the hard copy of your desk calendar is all," she replied, shoving the traitorous thoughts away.

"I see. Then you won't mind looking up."

She did. Mind. And she looked up. Only because not doing so would be childish. Soon as she made eye contact, however, she realized childish might have been the better alternative. Especially upon seeing the intense dark blue looking back.

"Much better," he said. "I'd like to speak with you in my office if you don't mind."

"About what?" She wasn't sure she wanted to know.

"My office, Elizabeth."

Feeling suddenly meek, she followed him in, taking up position in front of his desk while he hung up his coat. Another mistake, since the posture put her back to him.

"There's no firing squad," he said in her ear. His warm breath tickled her skin, causing goose bumps to erupt down her neck.

"Do you always have to do that?" she asked, swiping at her skin.

"Do what?"

"Sneak up on people."

"I don't 'sneak up' on people ever."

"Then you're a naturally stealthy walker."

"I'll take that as a compliment," he said, coming around her to the front of his desk.

"Take it however you'd like," she replied.

Standing face-to-face wasn't much better than having her back to him. Now her personal space not only had to contend with his citrusy scent but with the sight of his dark curls and freshly shaven skin. Her only saving grace was the pair of high heels she chose to wear this morning, that allowed her extra height. And even then, he still managed to make her feel petite and under his gaze.

She made one last effort to regain professional decorum. "You said you wanted to speak with me. What about?"

"This."

He kissed her.

The kiss wasn't passionate or hard and demanding. Quite the opposite. It was a quiet,
gentle touch of the lips. By the time Liz could
register what happened and react, the moment
was over. Leaving her off balance. "What...?"
Dazed, the words wouldn't form.

Charles smiled. "That's more like it," he
said, the back of his hand reaching out to
brush her cheek. "I thought about doing that
all night long."

"You did?"

"Uh-huh."

A thousand butterflies chose that moment
to take flight in her stomach. She pressed her
palm flat against her abdomen to quell them.
Suddenly fascinated by the artwork hanging
over his credenza, Liz walked toward it. "Do
you always feel the need to kiss your secretaries?"

"Only the tall, feisty ones."

"I see."

"You don't believe me."

She could feel Charles studying her and
imagined the narrowing of his blue eyes as
he tried to decipher the problem. She didn't
know what she believed. She was relieved to

know the attraction she'd felt passing between them was neither imagined nor one-sided. But knowing the attraction was mutual couldn't quell her uneasiness.

"Oh, I believe you. I'm wondering what made you think the desire was mutual."

"Because I know it is. Or would you prefer to keep pretending we're not attracted to one another." Once again, he'd found his way directly behind her.

"Dammit, I'm going to buy you some tap shoes," she whispered.

"I'm not the one who's tap dancing around the obvious," he said with a chuckle. His hands came to rest on her shoulders. "We're attracted to each other, Elizabeth," he murmured. "I didn't press the issue last night, but seeing you this morning, well…a part of me couldn't help itself."

Liz bit her lip, choking back the sigh that threatened to escape. Charles's touch was strong and comforting. The closeness of his body invited her to lean back against his broad chest. Offering support. Offering *more*.

"Couldn't help yourself, huh?" she heard herself saying.

"This wasn't planned, if that's what you mean. Nor was last night. I didn't come to your house last night with an ulterior motive."

"How did you—?"

"Your poker face. I could see the mistrust a mile away last night. I'm sure if I could see your face, I'd spy it again now. And I get why, too."

"You do?"

"Life is unfair. A person needs to protect himself."

Exactly. Relief began to wash over her, only to wash away. He understood because of experience. At the realization, a tightness wound its way around her chest and for a moment she wished she could let go and lean into his arms.

"You know those silly team building exercises?" she asked. "The ones where you fall backward and the other person has to catch you?"

"Trust falls?" She could tell he was confused by the reference.

"Can't do them to save my life. I wuss out every time."

"Hmm." Leaning forward, he managed to encroach on the little personal space she had left. "Tell you what," he said, his voice so silky and soft the words felt like a caress. "You let me know when you're ready to try."

left. "Tell your sister to wait." His voice as
stiff, and with the words Liz once released...
"You let me know when you're ready to try."

CHAPTER EIGHT

OVER the next three weeks Charles became a
fixture in the Strauss household. On Monday
and Wednesday he would arrive at six o'clock
sharp to help Andrew with his homework.
He always stayed for dinner, insisting he enjoyed Liz's no-frills cooking. Liz was pretty
certain the compliments were more out of
politeness since no one could possibly enjoy
meat loaf as much as he claimed. For his part,
Andrew appeared to be shedding some of his
sullenness. The other night, he and Charles
actually watched part of the hockey broadcast together.

On nights that Andrew played hockey,
Charles found his way to the games, bearing cups from the doughnut shop to "rescue"
her from the vending machine coffee, which
he called a travesty to coffee growers every-
where. His enthusiasm for high school hockey

wouldn't win any medals—but he did cheer at the appropriate times, and made a point to speak to parents who worked for him. With each game he attended his corporate approval rating increased. Liz wasn't surprised. When he wanted to, he could turn on the charm better than anyone, a fact she knew all too well. His silky voice was incredibly hard to resist.

A lot of things about the man were hard to resist, she thought with a guilty smile. She sat at her desk staring at her computer screen. Charles said he had a breakfast meeting so she was completely alone. She should be using the time to catch up on work, but her mind kept wandering over the past three weeks.

Although he made no bones about his attraction to her, Charles had been the perfect gentleman. At work and when tutoring Andrew, he kept his distance. But when Andrew left the room, he would steal sweet, semi-chaste kisses that would linger with just enough promise to make her insides melt with need. He never pushed for more; always letting her set the pace.

They were playing things safe. Correction, *she* was playing things safe. The growing sense of normal that surrounded seeing Charles at her dinner table or next to her on the bleachers told her she had to. Things were too good to trust they would last and far as she was concerned, life was hard enough. No need asking it to kick you in the teeth. Protect your heart; save yourself the fall.

"This overnight package arrived for Mr. Bishop. I told reception I'd give it to you." Leanne bustled into the outer office still in her red pea coat and boots. She read off the label. "Confidential. Interesting."

"Thanks." Liz took the package without comment. Her colleague was fishing for gossip again.

"Glad to help. By the way…" Lifting herself up, she rested her bottom on the corner of Liz's desk. Her boot heel tapped against the wood, the soft *thump* keeping time with the tapping of her index finger on her knee. "I wanted to tell you that whatever you're doing to your boyfriend, please keep doing it. Did you know he actually told the VP there was no rush to get him the next round of reports? *No rush.*"

"I told you, Leanne, I'm not *doing* anything."

"Right. Well, keep 'not doing anything,' because I like this new mood of his."

If Andrew were here, he would roll his eyes. Liz did the job for him. Leanne would believe what she wanted to believe, but Liz… Whatever was going on between her and Charles, she wouldn't presume to have any kind of power over him. The man would do what he wanted. If he told accounting there wasn't a rush, he no doubt had a very good reason.

Like the fact he wouldn't be here much longer. Her gaze flickered to the overnight package. Score one for playing it safe.

"Earth to Lizzie." A manicured hand waved in front of her face. "Is Andrew excited for tonight's game?"

Blinking, she nodded. "Can't wait." For the first time in years, Gilmore High School looked to win the state title. Tonight was the semifinal game. Fortunately, thanks to Charles, his grades had improved enough so he no longer had to worry about being benched. "Should be a good game."

"I'd love to see the kids win. They've played hard this year. Do you want me to save you and Mr. Bishop a seat?"

Again with the gossip. Liz shook her head. "You can save me one. I have no idea if Charles plans to go or not."

"Plans to go where?" The topic of their conversation walked into his office. Liz couldn't help but notice he had unusually bright eyes for so early in the morning. Whatever meeting he had must have gone well. Again, her gaze dropped to the package on the desk.

Leanne, on the other hand, jumped immediately to her feet. "Mr. Bishop! I was just delivering a package to Liz for you on the way to my office."

Silently Charles began to remove his gloves, one finger at a time. His eyes focused like lasers on the accounting secretary, their blueness probing as he waited for her to say something. Leanne smoothed the front of her coat. Then smoothed it again. "Which I've delivered," she said finally. "So I'll be on my way."

"Good idea."

"Was that really necessary?" Liz asked once they were alone.

"Good morning, Elizabeth, and yes. I like to keep people on their toes."

"Yes, we wouldn't want them to know

you're a nice guy." She couldn't help her smile. Leanne's fluster was amusing.

He smiled back. "No, we definitely wouldn't want people to think I'm nice, would we?" he drawled, leaning in so close she could feel his mint-scented breath on her lips. Her mouth ran dry. Would he kiss her here? In her office where anyone could walk in?

Instead he teased her by running the tip of his glove along her nose. "Now where is it Leanne is saving me a seat?" he asked, eyes sparkling.

"Tonight's Gilmore hockey game. The semifinals."

A shadow crossed his face, dimming the brightness. "I can't. I have a conference call this evening."

"Oh." Liz hated that her heart sank with the news. She had no reason to be disappointed. Just because he'd come to games in the past didn't mean he was obligated to come to every single one, or clue her in on his plans if he wasn't.

"I'm sorry," he said. As if he owed her an apology.

"No need." She thought she did a pretty

good job of sounding unaffected. "I'll let you know how they do."

Playoff games were always more popular than those during the regular season. Arriving at the Franklin rink, Liz couldn't find a parking place. She was forced to drive around the block several times and even after that, ended up snagging a space two streets over. Fortunately the weather gods had decided to bestow a midwinter thaw on the area, making walking the extra distance bearable.

Arriving at the crowded arena, she realized every student in all four grades from both schools had to be in attendance. The bleachers were jam-packed. Out of habit, she scanned the crowd for a familiar head of dark curls, getting halfway around before she caught herself. *He's not coming, remember?* He was back at the office waiting on an overseas call.

Leanne stood near the training room door. "Thought you were saving me a seat," she greeted the older woman. "What happened?"

"Playoffs happened. Apparently the opposing team has a very active booster club. It's standing room only. Best I can do is offer you a space here by the door. I can't see much, but since you're taller, you might have better luck. Where's your other half?"

"On the ice," Liz replied. Standing on her tiptoes, Liz spotted Andrew coming off the ice. He already looked sweaty and tired.

"I mean your boss. Is he parking the car?"

Dear Lord, but the woman didn't stop. "Contrary to what everyone thinks, we aren't a matched set," Liz told her. "We don't do everything together. In fact, Mr. Bishop is still at the office."

"He is?" Amazingly, even after what Liz told her, Leanne looked genuinely surprised. "I thought for sure he'd come tonight. Especially after—" The rest of her sentence got lost as two players smashed into the glass, causing the crowd around them to cheer. Liz quickly checked the numbers, saw that it wasn't Andrew and continued. "Especially after what?"

"Van and Doug told me he— Come on, Jimmy!" Looking to the ice, Liz saw Leanne's son make a terrific defensive play to save a goal. No sense pressing the woman any further. The names Van and Doug told her all she needed to know. There was some kind of new office gossip about Charles floating around, and as usual, those two were right in the thick of it.

Best she just watch the game and put all thoughts other than hockey out of her head.

She'd succeeded at the task pretty well, until the beginning of the third period when her senses began to tingle as though she were being watched. Scanning the crowd she saw no one. Then a familiar baritone whispered close in her ear, "Have I missed much?"

Liz jumped. Seeing Charles standing there, silly foam coffee cups in his hand, made her heart jump. "What are you doing here?"

"Hopefully watching Gilmore High School win," he replied. "I stopped at the doughnut shop on the way here. Would you believe there was a line?

"I think the truth about the vending machines has gotten out," he added in a low voice.

What she couldn't believe was the fact he was there. "What about your overseas call?"

"I rescheduled."

Liz coughed away the frog in her throat. Silly that his change of mind should get to her like this. It was only a high school hockey game for goodness' sake. So what if no one had ever rearranged plans for her in what felt like forever. "I didn't…"

"I know," he replied, not letting her finish. The understanding in his eyes shot all the way to her toes. "Drink your coffee before it gets cold."

Liz did as she was told and was mid sip when Leanne turned around to notice Charles had joined them. "Mr. Bishop!" she exclaimed. "You came after all. Lizzie said you couldn't make it."

"I had a change of plans."

The other secretary nodded with so much enthusiasm, her gold earrings slapped her jaw. Liz could imagine what kind of speculation was running through her head. "I'm so glad," Leanne was replying. "I wanted to say thank you in person. Van and Doug told me about your offer."

Charles waved her off. "It was the least I could do."

What offer? Liz listened with curiosity hoping the conversation would provide an answer but before Charles and Leanne could continue, a cheer erupted from the crowd drawing everyone's attention back to the few minutes of the game.

Gilmore won six to four. As the crowd filtered past them on the way out of the rink, Liz felt Charles's hand on her arm, his gentle grip pulling her close. "I don't want you to get trampled," he whispered in her ear.

"Seeing how I've got a good two inches or more on half the people here, I don't think that's a problem."

"Better safe than sorry." Though outwardly she rolled her eyes, the idea he was looking out for her secretly thrilled her. She felt delicate and feminine and dare she say, desirable? That notion thrilled her even more.

The crowd took a while to depart. Liz allowed herself the luxury of leaning back against his broad chest ever so slightly, not completely leaning on him but enough so she could feel his shoulder nudging between her shoulder blades. His temple hovered next to hers and while she nodded greetings to people passing by, the proximity allowed her to pretend the breath fanning her cheek was caused by a far more intimate embrace. When at last the crowd thinned, he released her, but the memory of his touch remained, along with the sensations it stirred inside her.

She looked over and, from the dark blue of his eyes, saw the closeness had affected him, too. "Did you really reschedule your call?" She needed to know he wasn't handing her a line. "Why?"

Charles shrugged. "It was a play-off game. I realized if the team lost, it would be the last time I'd have to watch them play."

The last time. Liz tried not to think about how those words settled so heavily. "I had no idea you'd become such a high school hockey fan."

"I like watching the crowd. Their passion is addictive." His eyes bore into her as he answered, the silent message unmistakable. The air in their tiny corner grew thick and clingy adding fuel to heat already running through her limbs.

Seeking to break the moment, she looked to the empty cup in her hand. "Well, the crowd is heading home now," she murmured.

"So it is." She felt the gentle pressure of a hand on the small of her back as he bid her to move. "Come on," he said, his voice husky. "I'll walk you to your car."

* * *

He led her outside, past a handful of fans sneaking cigarettes by the entrance and through to the rear of the parking lot. While they were inside, the sky had gone from starry to mottled gray and black clouds, taking away much of the warmth. Liz hardly noticed. The hand splayed against her back spread a warmth she could feel throughout her body. She combed her hair from her face, letting the night air wash the skating rink's staleness off her cheeks.

"Feels good, doesn't it?" Charles noted.

She nodded. "Though I'm sure the cold will catch up with me soon enough. Who knew a room with an ice floor cold get so warm?"

"Pack a couple hundred people inside and anything will get warm."

The ice rink was in a quiet part of town, near the high school and old town cemetery. As they walked in comfortable silence along the oak-lined sidewalk, past century old tombstones and family vaults, Liz was reminded of the old wives' tale. "Think we should whistle to ward off evil spirits?" she asked.

He drew her closer. "Don't worry. If anything bad is out there, I'll keep you safe."

The way he said the words, slow and deep, knocked on the walls around her heart and for a moment, she almost believed him.

A shiver invaded her thoughts.

"Cold's caught up with you," he said.

"Guess so." She didn't dare tell him the real reason she shivered was the way he made her feel.

"Hold on then." Stepping in front of her, he took the lapels of her overcoat and pulled them tight. A simple gesture, but it left Liz feeling cocooned in warmth and security.

"There," he said, his hands lingering, "we wouldn't want you to catch cold."

"Do you take this good care of all your assistants?"

"Only the ones I've kissed. Which, by the way," he added, letting his finger slip down the slope of her nose, "is a very, *very* short list."

"Good to know." Again, she almost—almost—believed she was special. Lord knows that right now, with the night air swirling around them and the heat of his body gliding against hers, she wanted to.

Switching gears, she returned to a question that had been nagging her since he arrived. "What offer was Leanne thanking you for?"

"I told Van and Doug I'd contribute the remainder of the funds needed to rebuild the ice rink."

"But that's…" Liz nearly tripped, she was so surprised. Fundraising efforts had only recently begun; last she heard, the balance needed was a sizable one.

Charles shrugged. "Makes for good public relations."

Except he looked almost embarrassed to have been found out. Hardly the reaction of a man seeking publicity for his good work.

Though she knew he wasn't looking for her approval, she gave it anyway. "I'm impressed."

If it was possible for a man's lashes to sweep over his eyes, Charles's accomplished the task. When he looked back at her, their color was softer, cobalt with a gratitude he need not feel as far as she was concerned. "Thank you, Miss Strauss. Your approval means a lot."

He was sincere and the fact her opinion actually mattered to him caused her entire body to fill with a warm glow. Suddenly everything about the night felt different. She felt different. Something had shifted inside her chest. A crack had formed in the wall, and her heart, so long protected, opened up.

Fingers trembling, she reached out and brushed them against his. Charles sucked in his breath at the contact, then a second later, she felt his fingers entwine with hers. "Do you need to give Andrew a ride home?" he asked.

She shook her head. "He has a date with Victoria. Why?"

A smile crossed Charles's features. A tentative, hopeful expression. "How would you like to taste a really good martini? Just a drink," he hastened to add. "No pressure."

This time the shiver passing through her was hot and left a trail of awareness in its wake. "I'd like that."

Charles's penthouse was located in a condominium complex on the banks of the Androscoggin River. Originally a textile mill, the cluster of buildings had been converted into residences a year before. She looked around with amazement. Sleek and modern, with ceilings at least fifteen feet high, the place was a designer's dream. The exposed brick walls blended seamlessly with hardwood and granite fixtures. Floor-to-ceiling windows, black as the night outside, reflected the furnishings like giant mirrors. Liz stepped off the foyer and found herself in a submerged pitlike area filled with an oversize sectional sofa. The focal point was a gas fireplace. A fireplace Charles lit by flicking a small switch on the wall.

"Wow. This is incredible." She was too blown over to say much more. Put her two-bedroom town home to shame, that's for sure.

And yet for all its gloss and opulence, the apartment felt empty. Like Charles's office, there were no photos or homey touches. No souvenirs from day trips. No clay handprints propped on bookcases. No books for that matter. The painting above the fireplace wasn't even hung; it sat propped on the mantel. An artsy way of displaying the work, but Liz couldn't help thinking the style had more to do with expediency. Charles could move tomorrow and it would take less than a day to pack his belongings. And most of that time would be for his wardrobe.

Liz's amazement dimmed a little.

"I keep the liquor in the kitchen," Charles told her.

He led her round the corner to a gourmet kitchen, which could house two of hers. "I certainly wouldn't trip over Andrew in this place," she joked only to realize how the comment sounded.

However, if Charles heard any presumption in her words, he didn't say anything. He was busy opening the oven door. "Shepherd's pie," he remarked, closing it again. "Told you my housekeeper had a fixation with ground beef."

Leaving the casserole in the oven, he crossed to the giant granite island. There he took out two glasses and a cocktail shaker from the cupboard beneath. "I'm pretty sure they had a basketball team in mind when they designed this place," he replied. "Too bad the average height in New Hampshire isn't six foot seven. Now, remember, I said it takes an artist to make a proper martini."

There was a bottle of gin on the counter. Not surprisingly Liz saw the brand was extremely expensive. "And are you an artist?"

"Not in the least," he replied with a straight face. "But I have practiced enough that I'm getting very close. First thing you have to remember is the mixing."

"Let me guess. Shaken, not stirred." The teasing note in her voice surprised her. She felt playful and it wasn't like her.

"Never." His eyes widened as if she suggested sacrilege. "Shaking bruises the gin."

"Oh," Liz replied. "We wouldn't want that."

"No, we wouldn't. I was referring however to the gin-vermouth ratio. The key is balance. You want just enough vermouth to bring out the gin's flavor but not so much as to overpower it."

Cupping her chin in her hand, Liz watched with fascination as he measured the duet of alcohol into the shaker. "I had no idea mixology was such a complicated science. Here I thought bartenders just poured liquor into a glass."

"And you would be wrong." He poured the drinks, dropped a toothpick-speared olive in each glass, and handed one to her. "Taste."

She did as she was told. Icy cold gin set her tongue on fire.

"This is where you say it's perfect, by the way."

"Okay," she said, taking another swallow. "It's perfect. Mahoney's can't come close."

"Told you so." He grinned, and Liz's insides did a little tumble.

Reminding herself the evening had no pressure, and needing to add a little space, Liz took her drink and headed toward the living room. In the pit area, the fire crackled invitingly. She stood before it and studied the glaringly bare mantel.

Charles walked up behind her. "Penny for your thoughts."

She had a dollar's worth. "Ever notice you can tell a lot about a person by their surroundings?" she asked him. "How they decorate. The items they leave lying around."

"Sure."

"I was thinking how I couldn't see any traces of your personality in this room. It's gorgeous, but it looks like something out of a decorating magazine. I don't see…well, *you* anywhere."

"Are you suggesting I'm hiding something?"

She shrugged, unsure what she meant. All she knew was that as beautiful as the room was, it made her sad. "Are you hiding something?" she asked.

"No. I simply believe in traveling light. No sense in dragging a lot with you."

If you didn't plan on staying. Made sense, but she wondered if there was more than just short-term living involved. This was, after all, a man who grew up in hotels. "What's your regular home like?"

"My regular home?"

"The one on the West Coast."

He stared up at the painting. "Pretty much the same. A little more furniture maybe."

But few personal touches. Same as this place. Quite a contrast from her, who'd saved every Popsicle stick decoration and souvenir from the last seventeen years. But then, he wasn't a man who valued intangibles, so keepsakes would hold little value.

"Makes for easy cleaning for sure," she mused. "Your housekeeper must be grateful…makes up for those windows."

She thought she kept a light note to her comment, but apparently not because he didn't smile the way she expected. In fact, he regarded her with a strange kind of seriousness.

"Let me show you something," he said after a moment.

Taking her by the hand, he led her across the room. Seeing he intended to lead her upstairs, Liz hesitated. Charles gave her arm a gentle tug. "It's not what you think. Come on."

Slowly she followed up, up and around the twisting stairs to the loft above the kitchen. Stepping up into the room, she gasped. It was like flipping a switch. Where downstairs was a pristine showplace, the loft was a paper-laden disaster. Reports, balls of discarded paper, newspapers, Sticky Notes, etc. littered the surfaces like some exploded office paper bomb. A pair of ties lay draped over the back of his desk chair, which was occupied by a stack of books so it couldn't be sat on anyway. In fact, the only thing not littered with paper was a large leather easy chair in the corner.

"Oh. My. Lord." Liz stifled a laugh. "You're a slob."

"Closet slob," Charles corrected.

"Still a slob."

A half full legal pad lay on the corner of the desk. Picking it up, she saw that an array of shapes and scribbles covered the margins. "Doodles?"

Charles blushed. She loved it. Seeing the

mess made her think the man who came to her house, the one who liked meat loaf and chicken dinners, was real.

That he was willing to share this room with her made her heart skip.

Setting the notepad down, she moved over to the other side of the desk, only to pause at the object in the corner. A scuffed baseball. It looked out of place among everything else. Running her fingers across the stitching, she looked at Charles questioningly.

"When I was around eight or nine, my father came out to San Francisco for an extended business trip. Somehow my mother heard he was in town, so she dumped me off at his hotel for the week. I forget where she and her boyfriend were going at the time.

"Anyway, most of the week I was stuck in the hotel room while he made sales calls."

"By yourself?" Didn't he say he was only eight?

"I was under strict orders not to leave the room under any circumstances. I was used to it by then so no big deal."

Sounded like one to her. Liz's respect for her former boss began to slip. This was a facet of Ron Bishop's personality she'd never known, yet it was strangely believable.

"What does that have to do with the baseball?"

"Apparently he told one of his potential customers about me, because the guy wanted to go on a father-son baseball outing."

"Ron was a sports nut."

"Yeah, and he had the misfortune of having a son who knew less than nothing about them. Still, I was excited to go and I caught a foul ball."

He took the ball from her and tossed it in the air with his free hand. "We had a good time that day. A real good time. Ron told me we'd go to another one next time he was in town."

"Did you?" She was afraid she already knew the answer.

The ball landed in Charles's palm with a soft plop. "Didn't have the time. Building a business takes work. I didn't really expect him to keep the promise anyway. My mother had already explained having me wasn't exactly in my father's plans. More like a failed gambit on her part."

"I'm sorry," Liz whispered. She didn't know what else to say.

"Don't be. I wrote both my parents off as lost causes a long time ago. The day I was accepted into Cal Tech, I said goodbye and never looked back."

Had he really? She studied the ball in Charles's hand. The lone souvenir carried along in a lifetime spent jumping from place to place. Thinking of a young Charles, holding on to the memory of one perfect afternoon, a piece of her heart broke away. His talisman wasn't so unlike what she'd been chasing in the backseat of Bill's car.

"Did you know your father had a heart attack?" she asked him. "I mean besides the one that killed him. Happened a few years ago. He had to have a quadruple bypass."

He was staring in the depths of his martini glass. "That's too bad."

"Afterward, he began acting a little differently. Company outings got more elaborate. We got better benefit packages. He took up golf. A lot of people figured his newfound zest was his way of cramming in as much life as possible after all those years building a business. That he regretted not enjoying his success earlier in life."

"What's your point?"

"I don't know. I wonder now if maybe he regretted more than working too much."

"You sound like his lawyer. He suggested the same thing. Then again he could also have simply wanted a person named Bishop at the helm of his legacy." Draining his drink, Charles set both the glass and the baseball back where it lay among the papers. "We'll never know what Ron was really thinking, though, will we?"

There was so much quiet bitterness in his voice, the last of Liz's walls crumbled away. Setting down her glass, she moved closer to him. Her fingers touched his cheek, stroking the faint stubble that lay beneath them. When she looked at his face, she saw eyes that were hooded and dark, the pupils blown so wide the blue was barely visible. His mouth moved to hers.

"No pressure," he whispered in a voice already low and thick.

"I know."

All their other kisses had been foreplay for this one. Liz moaned as Charles's mouth took hers. His lips were demanding, unyielding. He tasted of gin and coolness and heat. The woman in her cried out at being awoken at last, and she wrapped her arms around his neck drawing him closer. It was like throwing a match on a pile of dried kindling. Having ignited, there was no putting out the fire. This, she thought as Charles lowered her on to the floor, papers crinkling beneath their bodies, this was what she'd been missing for so long.

A few hours later Liz found herself back in her car, her body still burning. "Stay," Charles had asked as they lay together. The feathery touch of his hands on her thighs had almost made her say yes.

But she couldn't. She had a son to go home to. So she'd gotten dressed and kissed Charles good-night at the door. On the way out she spied a stack of papers on the entranceway table she hadn't noticed before. Documents from Xinhua Paper reminding her how Charles made his fortune. A cricket on her shoulder suggested she regret what happened, but she couldn't. She knew better than to expect promises or declarations of love from Charles and that was fine. And truth be known, she didn't want promises. She didn't expect love. Promises broke your heart. Love left you vulnerable.

No, she wouldn't be foolish enough to believe tonight had anything to do with love. The emotions lurking in the corner of her heart wouldn't take control. She would make tonight about pleasure. About allowing herself to be a woman for the first time in years.

She pulled into her driveway. The town house was dark except for a dim light in the living room. Odd. Andrew usually left every light on in the house, even when he went to bed. The kid was single-handedly keeping the power company employed. Looking in the rearview mirror, she checked her hair and makeup, hoping she didn't look too disheveled. Hopefully Andrew was in bed so she wouldn't have to come up with an explanation.

Dear God, she was sneaking around on her kid! What was she doing? The memory of Charles's firelight face hovering above hers quickly dissolved her rebuke.

Suddenly something caught the corner of her eye, and the moment was ripped away.

No… It couldn't be…Sure enough, there was Victoria's compact parked by the curb.

Her stomach sank. They weren't… They wouldn't…

In a flash she was out of the car and flooding the room with light before the front door had a chance to shut. Andrew leaped to his feet, his eyes bugged. His shirt was undone.

"Mom! You're home! I didn't hear your car."

"Obviously." Amazingly her voice remained calm. Looking to the sofa, she saw Victoria struggling to sit up and fix her blouse at the same time. Difficult with your bra unhooked.

Seeing where she was looking, Andrew stepped away from the sofa, presumably to draw her attention away. "Vic and I…"

"Were saying good-night," Liz answered for him. "You were saying good-night."

"Right." He held out a hand to assist his girlfriend. If she hadn't been ready to kill him, Liz might have considered the behavior gallant.

Silence engulfed the town house, the kids too mortified to talk in her presence. Good. Body stiff, Liz made her way to the kitchen.

Glaring at the cabinets, she waited till Andrew returned before speaking.

"Mom—"

"Don't." She cut him off. "Do you have any idea how furious I am with you right now? What were you thinking? Here? In our living room?"

"We weren't having sex."

"Oh, well then…" She yanked open the cupboard. "I thought I raised you to be more respectful—to be smarter."

"We are being smart. I told you, we weren't having—"

"Close enough," she shot back. "And maybe not this time, but what about next time, huh? Or the time after that! I'm not stupid, Andrew. How can you be so…" Dammit! She was so angry she couldn't talk straight. "For God's sake, you're only seventeen years old. What were you thinking?"

"You should talk," she heard him mutter.

Bad answer. Her stomach churned. She couldn't deal with this. Not right now. "Just go to your room," she told him. Her jaw hurt from gritting her teeth. "I don't want to see you till tomorrow.

"And leave the cell phone behind," she

added. No way was he going to sit in there texting.

Andrew immediately let out a disgusted groan. Acting as if he was a victim. "Oh, come on!"

"Now!"

"Fine." Thankfully he knew better than to argue. At least she had that going for her.

As soon as she heard the bedroom door slam, she grabbed a wine bottle from the cupboard. Her stomach felt as if someone had kicked a hole in the middle of it. Her baby boy...

We weren't having sex. She shook her head. The temptation was always one incredible kiss away. She knew all too well.

After all, Charles's scent was still on her skin.

CHAPTER NINE

UNBELIEVABLE. It was snowing again. Did the
stuff ever go away? He'd thought for sure last
night's thaw was a sign of improving condi-
tions. That was New England for you. Wait
five minutes and the weather would change.

Charles stared out his office window. It
wasn't snowing hard, but the clouds had
closed in over the mountains. He missed
them. The view had become part of his rou-
tine.

Didn't matter. He was still in a good mood.
Something had shifted inside him overnight.

He didn't have a name for it, but his chest
was full with the feeling. As if he'd gone to
the edge of the precipice and taken a plunge.
He felt amazing. Exhilarated.

Of course that might have more to do with
Elizabeth. Sweet, *passionate* Elizabeth. He'd

been with women before, but…wow. There weren't words to describe the experience. He couldn't get enough of her. Couldn't get close enough to her. It was like he wanted to crawl inside her skin and become a part of her.

God, listen to him. Eight-thirty in the morning and he was rarin' to go. Might as well be a teenager.

The ringing of his cell phone broke his thoughts. When he saw the number, he counted two rings and answered.

"*Ni hao ma*, Mr. Huang Bin."

On the other end of the phone, Huang Bin laughed. "Greetings to you. You sound quite energetic this morning. I take it your business crisis resolved itself satisfactorily."

"Yes, it did. Thank you for agreeing to re-schedule." Charles blamed his canceling on a business emergency. He didn't dare jeop-ardize negotiations by saying the emergency was a hockey game.

Even if his attending yielded amazing re-sults.

"Not a problem," the man on the other end replied. "This hour allows me to talk without interruption. I received your latest batch of financial information, and I must say we at Xinhua are quite impressed."

"I'm honored. Thank you."

"We believe it is time to move forward. I would like to take a tour of your facilities. To see for myself if your company is what we are looking for."

"Naturally."

"I will be in Boston at the end of the week for a symposium on Asian Trade. I would like to visit then."

Charles paused. "Did you say the end of this week?"

"Yes. Given how smoothly negotiations are going, I see no reason to delay, do you?"

"No, I don't." His good mood deflated slightly. He hadn't expected Huang to want to move this quickly. It meant he wouldn't have as much time with Elizabeth as he'd hoped.

Huang's voice sounded in his ear. "Charles? Are you there?"

"Yes," he said, recovering. "I'm sorry, you were saying?"

"I said that I would call you when I arrive in Boston. We can work out the time and date then."

"Sounds good. I'll talk to you at the end of the week."

They spoke for a few more moments, mostly small talk about family and weather and then Charles hung up. They were closing in on the final stage. If Huang liked what he saw it wouldn't be long before they hammered out the sale.

Immediately his mind traveled back to last night, and the experience he'd hoped to repeat as many times as possible. Damn. He washed a hand over his face. He didn't realize his time in New Hampshire would be ending so soon.

He wasn't sure he was quite ready to leave.

Standing in the doorway of Charles's office, Liz felt the heat from last night flare back to life. From the day he took over as her boss, she'd noticed how seriously he concentrated on his work, to the point that everything around him seemed to fade away. Back then she'd attributed the immersion to a form of tunnel vision, an inability to see beyond the numbers on the spreadsheet. She knew better now. She knew he channeled the same degree of attention to every task he sought to accomplish. Watching him clack away at his keyboard, she smiled remembering exactly how dexterous those hands could be.

Her smile faded. Memories were all she'd be experiencing from now on.

"Hey."

Her greeting came out so softly, she was surprised her voice was even audible. And in a way she half hoped he hadn't. This was not a conversation she looked forward to.

Unfortunately he looked up and smiled. "Good morning." To her dismay, his eyes held the same warm sparkle as they did last night. The gentle way he spoke, the way one was supposed to greet a lover, did not help, either. Both went straight to her chest, making her heart skip.

"How are you this morning?"

Simply marvelous. After Andrew stomped off to bed, she downed a glass of red wine, spent the night tossing and turning and woke up with a headache. Plus thanks in large part to the headache, not only did this morning's attempt at "talking" with Andrew fail, but her carefully made vows of maintaining perspective flew out the window when Victoria drove up. What's more, she didn't know what had her more worked up, catching Andrew or the fact that a mere hour before, she herself had lain in her boss's arms having what was, quite possibly, the most amazing night of her life.

"Fine," she lied in answer to his question. "You?"

"Perfect." Again with the lover's voice. All thick and lazy, it made Liz squeeze the door for support. He wasn't playing fair. A voice like that would make any woman weak in the knees.

He turned his attention back to the screen. "Do you know if Finance sent over the capital investment summary I asked for? I didn't see it in my inbox. I specifically told them to submit numbers to me today."

Good. He'd returned the focus to business. Business she could handle. "I'll call over this morning and remind them you're waiting."

"Remind them why, too." Closing his laptop, he rose from his desk. "Now," he said, zeroing his attention on her, "let us turn to more important matters."

Rising from his seat, he crossed the room, those eyes boring into her every step of the way. Liz's mouth ran dry. She'd forgotten the downside of his focus. You couldn't escape once caught in its sights. Eyes still locked with hers, Charles leaned forward and reached slowly behind her, his sleeve brushing the waistband of her skirt.

The office door clicked shut, closing the rest of the world out. "Good morning," he repeated. This time, he punctuated the greeting by pulling her in for a kiss. Much to her chagrin a tiny mewling noise escaped her mouth as she melted into him.

When he finished, they were both left breathless. Charles fanned his thumbs across her cheeks. "That's more like it," he rasped. "Much better than a boring old financial report." He pulled her close again.

Somehow Liz found the ability to back away. "We can't," she told him.

"Why not? If you're worried about getting in trouble at work, you needn't. I know the boss. And I promise I won't be filing an EEO complaint anytime soon, either."

She broke free from his embrace. It killed her leaving the warmth behind. "It has nothing to do with work," she told him.

"Then what is it?"

"I was thinking about last night…"

Charles leaned in a little closer. "So was I."

He wasn't playing fair. How was she supposed to put the brakes on anything when he insisted on talking like they were back lying in each other's arms? *Just spit it out, Liz,* she told herself. Go big or go home.

Crossing the room, she regained her personal space. "Look, I'm sure we both agree that what happened last night was…nice."

"Nice." His expression faltered a second, before reaffixing itself. "I would choose a different word."

They both knew she would, too. Like explosive or otherworldly. Squaring her shoulders, she pressed on, recalling the words she prepared earlier. "Regardless, given the circumstances, I think it would be best if what happened between us didn't happen again. We should keep things professional."

"I see." Crossing his arms, he leaned against the door. A dark, lean, unreadable pillar. "I hate to break it to you, Elizabeth," he said, "but that boat sailed a long time ago. Right around the time I first kissed you."

Liz blushed. He had a point.

Charles was studying her with confusion. "Has something changed that I don't know about? Because last time we saw each other, we were on the same page."

"I had some time to think, is all," she said, combing her hair back. "I'm not sure it's the best idea for me to be having an affair with you. I mean we have to work together."

"True. Although last time I looked, we also weren't the first people in the world to mix business and pleasure."

Did he have to draw out the word *pleasure*, giving it all sorts of connotations she'd rather not picture? "I mean I work *for* you."

"Again, we aren't the first so why don't you tell me the real reason for this sudden change of mind."

"Fine. It's Andrew." With that, she marched across the room, to his desk, purposely keeping her back to him for once, so she wouldn't be further distracted by his gaze. Breaking things off was a lot harder than she thought. Last night had opened a Pandora's box of feelings she was having trouble keeping under control. The minute she stepped into the office, every touch, every kiss had pooled hot and aching at the base of her spine.

Still, if she expected Andrew to keep his libido in check, then she should do the same.

"I need to think about what kind of example I provide him."

"If you ask me, you're providing him with a fantastic example."

"Not anymore," she whispered.

"Excuse me?"

"I said, not anymore." She sighed. "I walked in on Andrew and Victoria last night."

"Oh."

"Oh, indeed."

"Were they…?"

"He claims they weren't planning to go further than what I saw, but you and I both know in the heat of the moment, the best of plans mean squat." *After all, look at us last night.*

"I'm sorry. I know how worried you were something like this would happen." His hands suddenly appeared on her shoulders. Heaven help her, but they felt so comforting there. "Did you talk to him?"

"Sure, but it was a little hard making a strong argument when I'm wearing this." Turning around, she tugged at the collar of her shirt to expose the bruise in the hollow of her neck. "Now he sees me as a big hypocrite."

"Why, because you and I…? Elizabeth—"

he reached for her again "—he's seventeen years old. Surely he knows the difference between what a teenager does and two consenting adults who—"

"Who are having a short-term fling?" She yanked herself away before he could touch her and sabotage her resolve. "I'm sure he's going to see the logic in that sort of thinking."

"What makes you think this is short-term?"

He did not just say that. Did he think she was that big an idiot? "I know about Xinhua Paper, Charles. Are you really going to stand there and tell me you, America's most famous corporate flipper, are not negotiating to sell this company?"

His silence was enough of an answer. "I didn't think so. And if I get involved with you, all I'm doing is giving him permission to do the same. He's going to take one look and say 'Mom's having fun, why shouldn't I sleep with the girl I'm in love with?'"

She took a moment to calm down, hating for how badly she wished she could lean on him. "Look, I don't want him repeating my mistakes. I don't want to see him ruin his future."

"Like you did yours."

She nodded. "Yes. Last night was great but we both know it's not going anywhere, and I'm still raising my son. He may be in high school, but he still needs guidance. I can't afford to screw up. Please tell me you understand."

For several moments, Charles said nothing. Finally, however, he nodded. "I don't like it, but I understand. From now on we'll keep everything on a strictly professional level."

"Thank you." His acquiescence was exactly what she wanted, and yet disappointment he didn't argue the point stabbed her anyway. She suddenly felt quite hollow and alone. With the taste of regret in her mouth, she walked back to her desk. In the opposite direction she wanted to walk in. Behind her, she heard Charles taking a seat. "I'll go find out why Finance hasn't submitted those investment figures yet."

She closed the door to his office so she wouldn't change her mind and turn around.

"I'd like to propose a toast. Here's to Gilmore High School Hockey, runner-up in the Division Three State Championships!"

The crowd gave a lukewarm cheer, the sting of the afternoon's loss still hurt.

"Hey, what kind of attitude is that?" Van asked when his toast fell flat. "You guys made it all the way to the finals."

"Yeah and got smoked six to one," his son Sean replied.

"So you'll get them next year."

"Great, and since Andrew won't be there we can lose six-zip," another player said.

Watching from his seat across from Van, Charles took in the exchange with mild amusement. When Van asked him if he would join them after the game, his first inclination was to say no. With Huang coming tomorrow, he had a lot of work to do. Plus there was a business in Tucson he wanted his lawyers to look at. He really should call Jim Cavalier and get them to work. A hockey game dinner wasn't a priority.

But here he was for the same reason he rescheduled his conference call the other day. He couldn't pass up the chance to watch Elizabeth. Sure, he saw her every day at the office, but since their "breakup," their interactions had been kept on a strictly professional basis. Tonight was a chance to watch her while she cheered on Andrew. The way her face looked lit up with enthusiasm was too beautiful to pass up.

Of course, this evening wouldn't end quite as spectacularly as the last one because he was "respecting" her wishes and keeping his distance.

The effort was killing him. One night of lovemaking—not even one night—with Elizabeth was akin to one dose of drugs. Not nearly enough to knock her out of his system. His body craved more.

Then there was the fact he couldn't shake the feeling this thing with Andrew was only part of the problem. He couldn't stop wondering if she'd frightened herself by letting go and was using her son as an excuse.

Van tried again to get the team into the party spirit. "One more time, guys. Here's to Gilmore Hockey!"

At the other end of the table, Charles watched Elizabeth raise her soda and cheer with the best of them. "Mr. Hancock's right," she said. "You all should be very proud of yourselves for getting this far." She wore that sincere encouraging smile of hers, the one that when turned in your direction, made you feel like you could scale buildings. Seeing it, Charles realized it wasn't just the sex he missed. It was that smile, and the way she made him feel like smiling back. He missed sitting next to her.

He missed *her*.

At the table, Doug, Van and a few other people had started discussing what they considered a bad refereeing call in the first period. While they debated, Charles saw Elizabeth slip away to the bar with a pair of empty soda pitchers.

To hell with it, he decided. He wanted to talk to her. Grabbing a nearby empty tray, he pushed himself to his feet.

Elizabeth looked engrossed in the basketball game playing on TV when he approached, but her quick sidelong glance in his direction told him otherwise.

"I'm pretty sure those kids have eaten every boneless chicken in New England." The joke earned him a wan smile. It was a start.

"Great game," he continued. "Too bad they lost."

"Can't win all of them," she replied, eyes still glued to the set.

Was she talking about the game or them?

He wasn't always sure with her. "No, you can't. Doesn't mean you shouldn't try."

Studying her profile, he noticed for the first time how dark the circles were beneath her eyes. "You look tired."

"Busy couple of days. My boss is expecting an important visitor."

That wasn't why she was tired, though, was it? "I'm worried you're not getting enough sleep. I know I haven't been." His voice dropped so only she could hear what he said next. "My bed has been too empty."

"Charles..."

He took a mental step back. Hard as it was, he did promise. They fell silent. Forced to wait while the bartender filled her order, they both pretended to watch the basketball game. All he noticed were two teams running back and forth across a parquet floor. His attention was far too distracted by the woman next to him to attempt and learn what was going on.

Eventually he tired of the pretense and plucked a cardboard coaster from a nearby stack. "Lovebirds look like they're behaving," he noted, rolling the coaster square over end across the bar.

"So far anyway."

"How's that battle going?"

Liz shrugged. "The usual. I'm horrible because I insist on knowing his whereabouts and activities. I'm horrible because I won't allow him to hang out at Victoria's after school. I'm horrible because I exist. The usual."

Sounded harsh. "You okay with the attitude?"

"He thinks if he's obnoxious I'll feel bad and cut him slack. Things will blow over in a week or so."

"I wish there was something I could do to speed things along." Besides staying away.

He rolled the coaster up to her hand, letting the edge rest against the tip of her index finger. Touching her but not touching her. His hand twitched to trade places with the cardboard.

As if sensing his thoughts, she pulled her hand back. "Thanks, I'll be all right on my own."

"Alone being your favorite state of being and all."

She glared at him. "That's not fair."

No, it wasn't, but he only partly regretted the remark. "Life's too short, Elizabeth."

"And you're going to be leaving town in a

few weeks. Let's call it a draw." With a rough shove, she pushed the coaster back in his direction, a silent reminder she wasn't interested.

Realizing he wasn't going to get anywhere, Charles chose to take the hint and head back to the table. When he got there, he noticed one extra person. "Tim?"

Town manager Tim Callahan stood and shook his hand. "Glad to see you, Charles."

"Good to see you, too. What are you doing here?" He realized town hockey was a big deal, but showing up at a consolation dinner seemed a little excessive, and far as he knew Tim didn't know any of the families personally.

"I came by so the whole team could hear my announcement," the town manager replied. "Take a seat."

Still unsure what was going on, Charles sat down while the town manager stood up.

"May I have your attention, please," he called. "As you know, last summer the ice skating rink was struck by lightning and destroyed. We've been working on a replacement, but town funds have been limited. Fortunately, a private donor has stepped up and generously offered to pay for repairs and renovations."

The table cheered. "No more practicing in Franklin," Andrew said, fist pumping the kid next to him.

Charles looked to his plate and ground his teeth. So this is why Van insisted he be here. He didn't want them to make a big deal.

"Shortly after the donation was made, the fundraising committee came to the town with a request. The Board of Selectman voted in favor of it earlier this week and I'm here to announce that the new rink will be officially named the Charles Bishop Arena."

Again, the table cheered. Charles was stunned. "I don't know what to say." They were naming the rink after him? Him. Not his father. Warmth found its way to the center of his chest, melting the cold that had been there for so long and he felt like his chest would need to expand twice its size to accommodate the sensation.

"Thank you." He didn't trust himself to say anything more in case he choked on the uncharacteristic lump in his throat. "Thank you."

* * *

From her place at the bar, Elizabeth could see the back of Charles's head bow and issued a prayer of gratitude that she couldn't see his face. As it was, knowing he was no doubt struggling to maintain composure had her fighting her own battle. She wanted nothing more than to run to his side, to hold him as he rode out his emotions.

Seeing him today had been so difficult. She barely got through the workdays, and to be reminded of their time outside the office… Just knowing he was in the bleachers a few feet away was killing her. As much as she dreaded his departure, part of her was counting the days. Maybe then she could get rid of the longing that kept her up at night. These feelings he'd awakened were harder to put back in hibernation than she thought.

At least she could say she gave Charles some closure. He'd never know she'd been the one who suggested the name change from Ron Bishop to Charles. After hearing his story the other night, the change felt only fitting. Charles Bishop might not stay around, but he'd always know someone in Gilmore cared he was here.

CHAPTER TEN

"GREETINGS, my friend! It is good to finally meet you face-to-face." Entering the main entrance, Huang Bin clasped Charles's hand in a very Western handshake. "I am looking forward to touring your fine facilities."

"I think you'll be pleased with what you see," Charles replied. He took a good look at the man who would be the next CEO of Bishop Paper. The eldest son of a successful business dynasty, Bin was a handsome man with short black hair and a fit physique. He had a quiet arrogance about him that implied confidence and success. He was ruthless, unfailingly polite and, if rumors were to be true, exceedingly charming, especially when it came to the opposite sex. It was this last part that didn't sit well with Charles. He wasn't sure he liked the idea of Elizabeth's new boss being such a playboy.

"I must admit," Huang said as they walked to Charles's office. "When I first heard you were selling a paper company in New England, I was quite surprised. Based on your reputation, I did not expect to find you attached to an operation this small. But then I realized the connection. Your father started this company?"

"He did. About thirty-five years ago."

"A very admirable achievement. And now, following his death, you wish to capitalize on the fruits of his labor."

"I wouldn't exactly say capitalize." The word left a bad taste in his mouth.

"Do not fear," Huang replied, holding up a tanned hand. "I understand the desire to break free from one's father. I, too, inherited a company."

"I think you'll find Bishop Paper to be different from Xinhua in some respects."

"I have no doubt."

He pushed open the door to his outer office, allowing his guest to enter in front of him. Hardly surprising, Huang noticed Elizabeth at her desk straight away and smiled. She smiled back. Charles stepped in the space between them before opening his door. "You will find

our company is small and quite family oriented. It's something we pride ourselves on."
What was he saying, *we*? He couldn't care less.

"The company's size is one of the reasons we are interested," Huang replied. "We would prefer our first foray into North America to be a small scale."

Their conversation was interrupted by Elizabeth, who entered with a cup of steaming tea. Again Huang smiled. A little too brightly if you asked Charles.

An hour later Huang Bin was still in his office and still smiling. By now Charles had a headache. Huang had insisted Elizabeth join them on the tour—"To take notes," Huang claimed. He spent the entire tour forcing himself to remain cordial while convinced Huang was stealing glimpses at Elizabeth's long legs when he wasn't looking.

This deal, he thought, better be worth the effort.

"I am even more impressed than I was when I arrived," Huang said with enthusiasm. "You have a fine facility here. I can see what you mean about it having a family atmosphere. I was most impressed with the way you knew many of the employees personally."

"That is a byproduct of small town business. You find you cross paths with employees at a lot of events."

"How—" he searched for the word "—quaint. Do all the employees attend these 'events'?"

You mean *Elizabeth*, Charles wanted to ask. He wasn't sure he liked Huang Bin. The man was too much like an Asian version of himself.

"Depends upon the event, and the employee," he replied.

"I see. I look forward to learning the various activities."

"Then you would like to move forward?"

"Very much. With a few changes, I believe Bishop Paper will make a good acquisition and a good start to our North American venture."

"I beg your pardon?"

"Xinhua prefers a more streamlined production approach than you do in America. However, I believe we will be able to transition in time and keep most of the employees."

Most of the employees? "You're planning on layoffs."

"Some. It is inevitable I am afraid."

"But Gilmore is a one employer town. If you lay people off in this economy, they will have trouble finding new work."

"I sympathize with your loyalty and we will do our best to retrain. However, in the long run, a small work force will be required."

Layoffs. And after they'd named a damn ice skating rink for him. He felt sick to his stomach. "What am I supposed to tell my employees?" he asked to no one in particular.

"With all due respect, Charles," he heard Huang reply, "they will not be your employees for much longer."

They won't be your employees much longer.
Charles settled onto a bar stool at Mahoney's with a sigh. He couldn't bring himself to go home. As long a day as he had, he really didn't need to spend the evening in the apartment Elizabeth said had no personality. Layoffs. Damn. He knew the Huang family could be ruthless, but cutting jobs in Gilmore would be disastrous for the town's economy.

Layoffs never bothered you at any of your other companies.
They bothered him now. At other compa-

nies he didn't know employees' names. Last thing he wanted to see was people like Van Hancock out of work.

Elizabeth would be safe. Huang seemed more than interested in keeping her on board. Him and his unctuous smile.

He signaled for the bartender.

A pudgy man with salt and pepper hair and an armful of menus wandered over. "Welcome to Mahoney's, what can I get you?"

Charles ordered the ale. He was in a Twelve Weeks of Winter mood.

"Sure thing," the man replied. "Do you mind if we work around you while you drink? We got new specials to insert." He pointed to a stack of white paper.

"Knock yourself out," Charles replied. He wasn't in the mood to talk anyway. Not after an afternoon of being cordial to Huang.

This time he noticed the beer didn't taste quite so bitter. Either they'd tapped a new keg, and the heaviest flavor had sunk to the bottom, or he was acquiring a taste. Either way, the beer wasn't as bad as he remembered. Though hard to believe anything would be tasty without Elizabeth's company. She had turned out to be New Hampshire's brightest spot.

He slipped a page from the stack, wondering if the specials might be better, too. Out of habit, he ran a thumb across the stock, recognizing the grain immediately. "BishopLite," he said softly.

"What's that, mate?" the bartender asked.

Charles shook his head. "Quoting the paper stock, is all. It's BishopLite, fifty pound."

"You can tell from feeling it?"

Surprisingly he could. He'd been studying samples all week in preparation for his meeting. Nothing else to do since he couldn't study Elizabeth. "We manufacture it."

"Now I recognize you. You own the paper company."

"Did anyway. I made a deal to sell the place this afternoon."

"You don't sound too enthusiastic."

"Long day."

"Well, congratulations nonetheless." The man went back to changing out the menu folders, only to pause a second later. "Going to be weird not having a Bishop own the paper mill."

"Yeah," Charles caught himself saying. "It will."

The bartender was right. He didn't sound enthusiastic. By all rights he should be thrilled. He was finally rid of the albatross his father left him.

So why did he feel like he was leaving town with unfinished business?

Later he walked from the pub to downtown, partly to clear his head and partly because he was too restless to drive. Gilmore was a good-looking town. He'd been too young to notice when he lived here. The town common reminded him a little of a Christmas card with its walkways and snow-covered pavilion. If you stood at the far left corner, you saw a different view of his White Mountains. Funny, how he'd started thinking of them that way. That's what happens when you stare at something every morning. Or maybe he was simply developing fond feelings for the town. These past few weeks were the closest he felt to having a permanent home.

A short walk farther took him past St. Mark's where he attended probably his first and only pancake breakfast. His first, no second breakfast with Elizabeth. Terrible food, worst coffee. But it raised money for the ice rink.

The rink. He still couldn't believe they were going to name the blasted thing after him. He was going to insist if it bore his name it provide decent coffee. Maybe he'd make an additional donation to make certain. How ironic that he'd never have known about the rink—or Gilmore hockey for that matter—if not for Elizabeth wanting to watch Andrew, and the kid would never play there. He'd be off at Trenton next year. Kicking a block of snow that had broken onto the sidewalk, he watched as it broke into pieces. Least he'd helped Elizabeth fund that dream. Too bad their affair got snuffed before they had the chance to experience it fully. Instead he'd driven a wedge between mother and son and cost them all.

He stopped in his tracks. If he was going to leave Gilmore, the least he could do was fix what he broke.

Elizabeth's car wasn't in the driveway when he arrived at her town house. His chest felt a little hollow at not seeing it. He'd come to expect her smiling face to answer when he knocked.

This time, however, he hadn't come to see Elizabeth. The person he came to see was the young man who opened the door. "Mom's not here," Andrew said in a flat, tight voice.

"I know," Charles replied. "I came to see you."

"Me?" The kid flipped his hair from his eyes. When visible, you could see the resemblance to his mother's. "Why?"

"Because I think it's time you and I talked man-to-man, don't you?"

"About what?"

"Your mother."

Without waiting for an invitation, Charles let himself in.

News of the upcoming acquisition spread like wildfire. Charles had barely left the building when rumors started flying. By midafternoon Liz had received a dozen visitors all wanting to know the same things: when was Charles leaving and what did the change mean for Bishop Paper. Liz answered as best she could, but the truth was she didn't know any more than they did. That Charles was selling the company and Huang Bin was her new boss. She didn't like her new boss.

Leanne was among the first to come by looking for information. Not having seen them yet, Liz half expected the buzz birds to be close behind, but no. "I just heard the news. Does this mean you're leaving us?"

Making a production out of changing the toner in the copier machine so her colleague wouldn't spot her sudden mistiness, she was forced to pause when Leanne asked her question. That was one she hadn't expected. "Why would I be leaving?"

"When Mr. Bishop leaves of course. Are you going to be going with him?"

"No." She shoved the paper drawer closed as hard as she could. "I'm not going anywhere."

"Oh, sweetie, I'm so sorry. I know you were crazy about him."

She *liked* him, Liz wanted to correct, ignoring the warning bells the thought set off. They'd had a few good weeks spending time together and one really great night of sex. Nothing more. She was decidedly *not* crazy about the man.

Although she would like to know when he was leaving so she could be prepared. That is, so she could give people notice. All the speculation had left a gaping hole in her chest. On the plus side, the pain reminded her she'd done the right thing to break it off. If it hurt this badly now, imagine what she'd feel like if she'd truly had time to fall. Thank goodness she protected her heart.

By four o'clock, Liz had had enough and drove home. If Charles could take off early without word, so could she.

Immediately upon seeing the familiar car in the driveway, Liz's heart stopped. What was he doing here? She marched her way to the house curious to find out. The front door was left open. She was halfway through the opening when she caught Charles and Andrew's conversation.

"So you see why she's going a little overboard, don't you?"

Dear God. She pressed her palm to her mouth so they wouldn't hear her gasp. Was he talking to Andrew about what happened?

"Yeah," she heard Andrew say, "but does she have to be so crazy?"

"Can you blame her after what she walked in on? Your mother wants you to have the best possible future. It's what makes her special."

"I know."

"Trust me. Your mom's awesome. My parents didn't give two squats about me."

Liz's palm curled into a fist, which she jammed to her lips. For some reason Charles decided to take it upon himself to talk with Andrew. Why would he go and do something like that? An emotion shook itself loose. A scary, powerful emotion she didn't want to feel. He shouldn't have done this. She had the situation handled.

Squeezing her eyes shut, she packed the reaction away before shutting the door as loudly as possible. "I'm home," she called, faking an upbeat greeting.

"Hey, Mom!" Andrew called back.

Wearing her best faux smile, she made her way into the living room. "Charles, what are you doing here?"

"Talking to Andrew," he replied.

"Is that so?" She looked at them both, waiting for further details. Instead she witnessed a conspiratorial look passing between them.

"He wanted to talk about calculus," Andrew told her. "To make sure I'm okay now that he's not tutoring and all."

"How nice of him."

"Yeah, it was really helpful."

It took all her effort to nod and pretend her son wasn't lying to her. "Do you mind if I talk to Mr. Bishop alone?"

"No." The teenager unfolded himself from the sofa. "I'll see you later, Mr. Bishop."

To her amazement, Charles held out his hand. "I'm glad we sorted things out, Andrew."

"Me, too." Grabbing his cell phone from the coffee table, he pounded his way upstairs. A few seconds later, his bedroom door shut.

Liz opened her mouth to speak, but Charles beat her to it. "How much did you hear?" he asked, sauntering toward her.

"Enough to know you weren't talking about calculus. What were you doing?"

"I wanted to clear the air with your son." He coughed. "Since I'm partially to blame for this cold war you're having."

"You shouldn't have," she replied.

"I wanted to."

"I mean, you shouldn't have."

"And now you're upset." Ignoring the arms she'd folded across her chest as a blockage, he leaned forward and caught her chin with his thumb and forefinger. "Why?"

"Because I don't need you to come run-

ning in to my rescue just because he and I
are having a disagreement." She broke away
from his touch, hating how her body instantly melted at his touch. Even now, her
skin burned where he touched her. "I can handle this on my own." In the back of her mind,
a tiny voice questioned her real reason for
being stubborn after accepting all of Charles's
other help. She was afraid to answer. Afraid
to admit the truth.

"I know you don't need my help with this
issue," Charles told her. "But I don't like leaving loose ends."

"Is that what I am, a loose end?" Sounded
about right.

There was no mistaking the regret in his
eyes as he traced the back of his hand along
her cheek. He studied her face for a long time
until the regret became muddled with a new
and different emotion. One that Liz couldn't
name or rather was afraid to, because seeing
it made her heart start to race uncontrolla-
bly. For a moment, he looked about ready to
speak, but his lips moved without words. It
was as if he were trying to form the thoughts
and failing.

In the end, he simply stroked her cheek a

second time, drawing out the contact for as long as possible while his brow furrowed in confusion. "Goodbye, Elizabeth."

He left her standing alone in her foyer.

That night, Charles sat in his study staring at the ball on his desk. The loft reminded him of Elizabeth these days. Hell, everything reminded him of Elizabeth, even the baseball. From now on he'd forever associate it with the night the two of them shared. The most incredible experience of his life.

The first time he shared part of his past with someone.

He still didn't know what prompted him to open up like that. For all intents and purposes, sharing personal information with someone was illogical and poor business practice. But Elizabeth made him act out of character. Hell, he actually had a heart-to-heart with a teenager because of her. Which didn't go all that bad, once they got started. He'd never qualify as a fifties sitcom father, but he did all right.

With a long sigh he set down the ball and picked up the report he'd been searching for. The original green initiatives proposal. He smiled, thinking of how easily Elizabeth rattled off facts and figures at the meeting in Concord. Sitting there in that ugly reindeer sweater, looking like a damn cover model. Looking back, he'd been a goner the minute she lectured him outside the restaurant.

A goner. His heart stilled. Was it possible? Elizabeth's face danced before him. He pictured her eyes. How they could be soft and light like hazelnut one moment and dark like chocolate the next. How they could turn black with desire or flash white-hot with determination.

How they could make you feel ten feet tall with their sparkle.

An ache locked itself in his chest. He finally understood why this sale bothered him. He hated the idea of leaving Elizabeth behind. He hated the idea of leaving her at all.

Of losing her.

The emotion that had plagued him for days finally had a name. Breaking free, it spread through his limbs and into his heart, filling him with a certainty like never before. He wanted Elizabeth. He wanted home cooked meals and high school hockey games and calculus homework. He wanted martinis and doughnut shop coffee and risking his life

hitting deer. What he didn't want was to leave
Elizabeth.

He was in love with his secretary.

The next morning Liz was sitting at her
desk trying to pretend yesterday never happened. That Charles had not stopped by her
house to talk with Andrew. Try as she might,
she couldn't get the look on his face out of
her mind. Something about his expression
wouldn't let go and the power frightened her.
She wanted nothing more than to bury herself
in work for the next few weeks.

"Good morning, Elizabeth."

Would she ever hear Charles's greeting and
not feel a reaction? Looking up she saw him
standing in front of her with a smile brighter
than any she'd ever seen.

Rather than speaking, he pulled her into his
arms and kissed her. A hard, passionate kiss
that left her shaking and clinging to his coat.
When she finally had the strength to move
her forehead from his, she wished she hadn't.

What had been a hint of vague emotion
in his eyes yesterday was now brilliant and
certain. Its vibrancy called to her very core,

wrapping around her heart and filling it with promise.

It scared the hell out of her.

"What if I told you I've decided not to sell Bishop Paper?" he asked her.

"I don't understand…."

Smiling, he brushed the hair from her cheek. His fingers were cold from the weather, and yet she was certain the temperature wasn't the cause of her shiver. "I've decided to stay in Gilmore."

Stay? He was staying? She'd been so certain his existence in her life would be temporary.

"But…"

He pressed an index finger to her lips. "I did a lot of thinking last night. I couldn't figure out why this sale didn't feel the same as the others. Normally by now I'd be ready to move on, knee deep in my next business acquisition. But I haven't even looked. I hadn't even thought about looking. You know why?"

Too stunned to speak, Liz shook her head.

He cradled her face in his hands so she had to look in his eyes. "The past month has been the most amazing month of my life. For the first time, I felt like I was a real part of something. That I had a place I belonged. I want to hold on to that feeling."

"By staying here at Bishop." Her head started to swim. The air wouldn't go into her lungs, making her dizzy.

And still Charles kept smiling, his eyes resplendent in their blueness. "No, I mean staying with you. That's what I realized last night. Every good memory I have of this place involves you. You are the reason I want to stay, Elizabeth. I love you."

I love you. Liz's insides froze. She should be thrilled. This is what she was supposed to want, what she told herself not to hope for, and here it was happening. Why wasn't she overjoyed? Why did her entire body feel numb? Her heart began slamming against her rib cage. The room started to close in on her.

She pushed her way from his arms, to the other side the room where she could think.

"Elizabeth?" He came up behind her. "What's wrong?"

What was wrong was he'd said he loved her! "You can't love me," she told him, staring at the wall.

"Why not?"

"Because." God, what she would have done

to hear those words once upon a time. What she did do to hear them. "I used to dream those words meant forever."

"They still can," he said, trying to draw her into his embrace.

"No," she said, fighting him. "That dream died a long time ago. I'm not sixteen and a half anymore. Dreams don't have the same appeal. Even if you get them, they fall through. Companies get sold. People leave. And believing they won't only leaves you worse off than before." That was the real bottom line. She'd loved and been stomped on enough in this world. She wasn't going to be stupid enough to try again.

"So, what?" he asked her. "Better to be alone than risk love and lose?"

"Why not?"

"Because it's a load of bull crap, that's why."

Liz blinked at the word. "Bad things happen all the time, Elizabeth. Life can kick you in the teeth. That's no excuse to not live."

"I live."

"No, you live through your son. That's not a life. That's existing."

She whirled around. "Don't you dare judge

my decisions. I'm not the person who came here intending to obliterate his father's legacy."

"You're right." He met her toe-to-toe, his jaw tight with emotion. "I came here and I hated the man. I wanted to wipe his stupid company off the face of the map. And I'm not going to deny that I'm still angry, either. But you know something?" His nostrils flared. "I also figured out that getting rid of my father's memory wasn't going to fill the emptiness in my chest. That could only be filled by being part of something."

"For how long?" Liz countered.

"What?"

"How long will you be a part of this great something? I turned you down. There's no reason for you to stay. How long before you find a new buyer?"

Choking back what sounded like a groan, Charles jammed his fingers through his hair. "Why can't you believe I simply want to be here for you?"

"Because no one has before!"

The confession tore through her, coming out like a shot. She stood, fists at her sides, waiting for his reaction. For the inevitable admission she was right again. For him to back away from her like Bill and her mother.

But to her surprise, he didn't. "I'm not like the others," he said in a quiet voice. "The only one running is you."

CHAPTER ELEVEN

Liz sat in her car in the darkened driveway telling herself she did not run away. She protected herself.

It was a lie.

I love you. What was wrong with her? An incredible man tells her he loves her, and what does she do? She should have thrown herself into his arms and told him the truth. That she was in love with him, too. Because she was. Much as she wanted to deny the truth, her heart knew otherwise. And yet instead of running toward him, her feet sent her the other way.

She was an idiot.

Andrew was already home and playing video games when she finally found the energy to walk into the house. Soon as he saw her, he dropped the controller. "Did you get my text?"

"What?"

"My text? I sent you one about an hour ago. My acceptance to Trenton came today."

Though hard, she managed an enthusiastic smile. "That's great, honey."

"They sent a whole bunch of financial aid stuff, too. I left the papers on the dining room table."

"Thanks. I'll look at them after dinner. Do you want to invite Victoria over to celebrate?"

"Sure. Do you, um…" He worried his bottom lip in his teeth. "Do you want to invite Mr. Bishop?"

Liz winced. "I don't think so."

"Why not? I thought you guys were having a, you know, a thing." With nonchalance she could only wish for, he retrieved the controller and returned to his game.

"Not…" Might as well be honest with the kid. "Not anymore."

"Is it because of me?"

"No."

"Mom…" He turned off the game. "Charles came by and talked with me. He told me you were worried that you'd give me the wrong impression and how upset you were with me and Vic."

"I know. I overheard part of the conversation."

"Figured you did."

She really didn't fool anybody, did she? "So, you want to tell me what he said?"

"I already told you," Andrew said with a shrug. "We talked about Victoria and how much you wanted me to have all the opportunities you missed out on, and how his parents pretty much ignored him growing up. Said he wanted me to appreciate how lucky I am. I do, you know."

She ruffled his hair, getting an annoyed head jerk. "Thanks," she said with a smile.

"He's not a bad guy really. I mean, he's a little stiff and he likes math a little too much, but just so you know, I'm cool with you dating him."

"I appreciate the permission." More than he'd know. "But I don't think that's going to happen."

"How come? It's clear he likes you."

"Yeah, he does," Liz replied, looking at her hands.

"And you like him, so why not hook up?"

"It's complicated."

Her son looked at her with a seriousness

that made her realize her little boy wasn't so little anymore. "Not really. Not if you're into each other."

Later that night, Liz sat in the dark and thought about what her son said. Was it really as simple as allowing Charles into her heart? She was too old to rebuild her life again if it fell apart.

But what if it didn't fall apart?

A stupid question. Things always fell apart. Was whatever happiness you eked out worth the pain of eventually losing everything?

Rolling onto her side, she listened as Andrew got ready for bed. She was so proud of him for getting into Trenton. Her baby boy. He'd grown into such a great young man. She wouldn't trade him for the world.

Even though he's going to leave you?

Her insides stilled as the double standard smacked her square over the head. She loved Andrew with all her heart and soul, and though she knew he would leave her someday, she didn't regret one minute of having him. Far as she was concerned, the only person who lost out was his father. Her son had been worth every ounce of pain, sacrifice and fear.

You're living through him. That's not living. That's existing.

Rolling onto her back, Liz stared at the ceiling.

So maybe grabbing a little personal happiness would be worth the risk?

What if it fell apart?

What if it didn't?

Liz sighed. She wished she knew for sure.

Staring out into the parking lot, Charles couldn't help feel a tiny grain of relief. For the first time in what felt like months, Charles could see grass. Granted it was brown, but the promise of green and rebirth existed.

He wished he could say the same for his relationship with Elizabeth. They were still at a frozen impasse. Originally he'd hoped, after talking to her, she might see things differently, but as the night stretched out into morning, that hope began to fade.

Maybe she was right. Maybe forever was a big fat fantasy.

Go big or go home. Liz pressed a palm to her abdomen and knocked softly on the door.

"Come in."

Charles stood with his back to her, watching out the window. She wished she knew what he found so fascinating about the parking lot, but no matter. He looked so perfect standing there, her heart automatically flip-flopped.

"Hey," she greeted in a soft voice. "Can I have a word with you?"

He turned, and her breath caught. Wasn't fair a man could have such beautiful eyes. Nor was it fair they looked so sad.

Because of her.

"What can I do for you?"

Where did she start? "About yesterday. What you said…"

He waved her off. "I was out of line. Forget it."

"No. I can't. You were right."

He stared at her. "What?"

Now or never. "I'm scared."

There. She'd said it. "I'm scared that I'll finally be happy and life will pull the rug out from under me. That I'll end up lost and alone and worse off than ever. I wasn't sure I could survive losing something really wonderful. And you are the most wonderful thing that has happened to me in a long, long time.

So I buried my heart as deep as I could and told myself I could fall. Because if I did, I'd crash and burn."

She paused. Charles didn't say a word so she plunged onward.

"Even now I'm afraid I'm making a mistake. I mean, I thought I'd be fine if I stayed alone. That I wouldn't get hurt, but…but…" Voice cracking, she sniffed away the emotion. "I'm pretty darn unhappy right now. So maybe the excuses are just as bad. Maybe I wasn't protecting my heart after all."

Again, Charles said nothing. Liz's heart sank. *So much for taking a chance.* She'd waited too long. She'd pushed him away one too many times.

Dejected, she turned to leave. "That's all I had to say. I just wanted you to know that when I said no, it wasn't because of you. And I'm sorry if I made you think it was."

"No one ever said life came with guarantees."

She stopped. "I know."

"I can't promise you a lifetime of never ending happiness, Elizabeth, or that there won't be problems and bumps in the road. I don't know what tomorrow will bring.

"The best I can do," he said, coming up from behind her, "is promise to try my damnedest to see that the ride is as wonderful and smooth as possible. The rest, you simply have to take on faith."

She let his words wash over her. Amazingly they were the most reassuring promises she'd ever received. "Faith, huh? I think I could try."

"Really?"

Starting now. Squeezing her eyes tight, Liz relaxed. And fell backward.

"Whoa! What the—"

She tumbled into Charles's waiting arms. Opening her eyes, she smiled at the man gazing down. His eyes bright with more emotion than she thought possible.

"You caught me," she said, touching his cheek.

He kissed her palm. "And I will every time. I love you, Elizabeth."

At that moment, Liz knew that no matter what happened in her future, this moment was worth every chance she took. "I love you, too," she told him, pulling him down for a kiss. "I love you, too."

EPILOGUE

"Mom!"

At last. The salon promised the mousse would give the style lift, and for once in her life, her hair was volumized and behaving.

"Mom!"

The door to the ready room burst open. Liz smiled at the young man in the doorway. Dressed in his black tuxedo, the Trenton alum and new college freshman looked like a million dollars. Tears of pride sprang to her eyes. "You look so handsome," she told him, smoothing his lapels.

He brushed away her aggravation. "Mom, hurry up."

"Just a minute. I need to catch my breath." About a thousand butterflies had just taken flight in her stomach.

"Now, Mom. Everyone's waiting."

"Fine," she replied, sighing. She'd remember this next time he asked for a little more time. "Do you know where—"

"On the table by the door."

"Oh, right. Thanks."

Hands shaking, she hooked her arm through his and let him lead her out. "How do I...?"

"Great, Mom." Andrew paused and smiled, giving a glimpse of the man he would someday be. "You look beautiful. Now, let's get this show going."

The doors opened, and a hundred faces turned to look at her. Liz didn't notice. Her eyes were focused on the man standing at the front of the church. Charles wore a smile brighter than any light.

Instantly the butterflies in her stomach stopped. This risk, she thought, would be a piece of cake.

On the arm of her son, she headed down the aisle toward her future husband. The man who would always catch her when she fell.

* * * * *

LARGER-PRINT BOOKS!

GET 2 FREE LARGER-PRINT NOVELS PLUS
2 FREE GIFTS!

Harlequin *Romance*

From the Heart, For the Heart